Joshua

THE WHITFIELD RANCHER BOOK 3

KATHI S. BARTON

This is a work of fiction. Names, characters, places, and incidents are products of the author's imagination or are used fictitiously and are not to be construed as real. Any resemblance to actual events, locations, organizations, or persons, living or dead, is entirely coincidental.

World Castle Publishing, LLC

Pensacola, Florida

Copyright © Kathi S. Barton 2018

Paperback ISBN: 9781629899282

eBook ISBN: 9781629899299

First Edition World Castle Publishing, LLC, May 14, 2018

http://www.worldcastlepublishing.com

Licensing Notes

Cover: Karen Fuller

Editor: Maxine Bringenberg

Table of Contents

Chapter 1

Carter didn't move as she sat in front of the desk. Today was her fourth day out trying to find a job, and the second time that she'd been asked to wait while they checked on something. While she knew what they were checking on, calling the police to find out if her story matched what they were told, they had no intention of hiring her.

"Miss Compton, I have a buddy that will hire you." She looked at the administrative assistant who'd came in when the boss left her alone. "He's a good guy. He and his brother are opening a greenhouse and they're hiring a lot of people."

"I have to find me a job or go back to the halfway house." The woman nodded and smiled as she handed her a piece of paper with a name and address on it. When their fingers touched, Carter looked at the woman. "Don't go home at lunch. He'll kill you if you do."

Startled, the woman just stared at her. "He's having an affair." Carter nodded. "I thought so. So, if I don't go home for lunch, what happens to me and my children? We have to have someplace to live now that he's out fucking his secretary."

"If you trust me enough not to go home at lunch, it'll all be cleared up and you'll be safe." The woman stared at her for several seconds, and only stood when her boss returned. Carter nodded when she did. The boss, however, wasn't pleased.

"You should know that we are a nice reputable company, and don't condone having convicts working here." She didn't even bother telling her that she had been exonerated of all charges. Standing, Carter started walking toward the door. "You should have known not to come in here looking for a handout either. We don't do that. Now, I'd like for you to leave."

Carter could have told the secretary that her husband was also having an affair with the man that did their books for them. She could have told her that her nice company that didn't deal with convicts was making meth for the local drug lord down the block, but didn't do that either. Instead, she left there without saying a word.

If the woman didn't go home for lunch, which she didn't think that she would now, the two people in the bed would be killed by the man who cooked the books for her husband and was his part time lover. Not only that, he'd kill himself too while he was there. It would be a mess, but the woman would be able to get her insurance on her husband and a very nice settlement from the man's insurance. She would be safe with her children from now on.

Walking in the bright sunshine, she made her way back to the apartment her sister had set up for her. Her friend was there, Dylan Whitfield, and Dylan's sister-in-law, Sunny. They had been here for two days with an elderly man and didn't seem inclined to go home without her and Rachel. Carter looked at the same elderly man as he came toward her on the sidewalk.

"You get the job?" She told him that she'd not. "Didn't think you did. Some people aren't as forward thinking as I am. I've come to take you to lunch. And then you and me, we'll have us a nice conversation."

"Mr. Whitfield, you guys would be much safer if you just left me here. I know what I'm doing." He said he knew that too. She was smart, he told her. "It's not that. You don't know what I'm capable of."

"Is that why you won't let me touch you? Or anybody for that matter?" The man was smart as well, but she had been at this a lot longer than he had been guessing. "I noticed that right away. When someone gets too close to you, you back up fast and far. Leaving your hands in your pockets all the time too, that's so nobody will try and shake your hand. What can you do? Read minds and the such?"

"Yes, and the such is much worse." He nodded and opened the door to the little deli that he'd led her to. When they were seated, she looked at him. "I'm able to do things that you've never thought of. I see things that people don't need to know. I could kill a person halfway around the world and never touch them. I won't if I don't have to, but if it came to protecting my sister and myself, I would in a heartbeat."

The waitress took their order, Ollie ordering for her when she wouldn't. Then when the waitress was gone, returning once with their drinks, he stared at Carter but didn't say anything for long moments. She didn't squirm or get nervous. This was a good man, and she had no reason to fear anything about him.

7

"Rachel said she won't go without you. Can you make her go?" She said that she could but would rather not. "You lift things up too, don't you? Not just little, but big stuff too."

"Yes." Her answer was short, but that seemed to be all he required for now. Their salads were set in front of them when he looked around the restaurant. Then when he looked at her, she could see determination in his eyes.

"Who's coming for the two of you? Can you tell me that?" She told him who was coming and why. "Your parents, they want you for bigger things. I'm guessing for some of them abilities that you're not talking about."

Again, she gave him the short answer and he nodded. Eating the salad, she thought about what this man knew that she'd not even shared with her sister. And there was plenty more that he didn't know. Or, and this was likely most of it, he was afraid of asking her.

"I want you to come back home with me. Now hear me out before you tell me no. Your sister, she ain't going if you don't, and even though you can make her, I got it in my heart that it won't do you no good to send her to my place, because your parents will take you and that'll bring her back here." Carter asked him if he'd stop Rachel. "No. I know about family and the ties that bind. She ain't gonna stop trying until she wears me plum out. Then she'll be hurt anyway, or killed. When they coming, these so-called parents of yours?"

"You believe me." He said that he had no reason to think that she'd lie to him. "Mr. Whitfield, I've been in prison for the last ten years. I'm sure that you know convicts better than that."

"I'm gonna tell you again to stop calling yourself that. You got out because they just figured out that you didn't do those things they said about you. That don't make you a convict, that makes you a victim. And while I know you can take care of yourself—I don't doubt that one bit—that sister of yours, she's not going to be so easy to protect with knowing you're out here all by your lonesome."

She looked around the restaurant, then back at him. "The man over there with the woman in green—he's having an affair with her. Not because he wants to, but she's his boss and she's making him. His wife knows now, he confessed it all to her, and she's going to try and kill her. But she accidently kills her husband instead, and three lives are ruined." He asked her if she could stop that from happening. "Yes, I could, but there are repercussions to doing that. If he is set to die, then something else will happen that will kill him. Maybe not today, but soon after. His wife isn't a good person either, but she loves her husband and the money that he makes. So instead of just talking, as they should, she'll take matters into her own hands."

"There are other stories you could tell me about the people here. I'm sure that you could tell me about myself too. I don't want to know nothing, by the way. But I do know that if you don't come along with your sister, she will be killed, and you'll end up killing your parents. Is that something that you could live with?" No, she told him, Rachel had been good to her. "But your parents you don't care about?"

"No, not at all." He nodded, and when her burger with fries was set in front of her, she looked at the man who in the last few days had been kinder to her than anyone, except for her sister Rachel, had been in a decade. "I'm not a person that people like. I'm very prone to being nasty, and sarcastic too."

"I like you. Very much. You're a good deal smarter than

you let people know about. You have a sense of goodness about you that no one sees. You're witty and funny. I get peeks of it occasionally, that humor that you hide, but you got one." Carter just smiled at him. "There it is, that pretty smile you got. What do you think of my deal?"

"All you said was to come home with you to make sure that Rachel was safe. While I don't have restrictions on where I can go and work, I do need a job so that I can stop sponging off my sister. She sold everything so that she could try and take me to Dylan and your family, and I don't want her hurting for that." Ollie told her that he'd give her a job. "I'm not a puppy that needs for you to take care of me."

"Don't care all that much for dogs, me being a cat and all, but I like the wolves on my property and that of my grandsons. The wolves, they're out to protect us when they can. We do the same for them." She took a bite of her burger and moaned at it. It was the first one that she'd had in ten years, and it tasted so good. "You come on home with me and I'll make sure you get fattened up with food like that all the time. My daughter-in-law, Eve, she can bake a pie that'll make you sing her praises to the heavens."

"Ollie, I'm trying very hard to save you and your family from all this. You're making it very difficult to say no to you, and you have to know that I have to stay here." He said he understood that, but she could use a backup, everyone needed that. "You do understand that I'm a good deal stronger than the wolves and your family as tigers, don't you?"

"You might be able to lift up a car and make it twirl in the sky, but you ain't that strong when it comes to somebody loving you." Carter looked away, unable to say anything around the lump in her throat. "You come home with me, darlin' and I'll show you a whole passel of people that will love you like you deserve. And I'm thinking of all the people that I know, you need to be loved more than most."

"You could be hurt. Perhaps even killed by this." He said that he'd been hurt before. "But they're coming, Ollie, and they mean to get what they want at all costs."

"So do I. I mean to save you the same way, if you'll let me."

Walking out of the little restaurant, she didn't tell him yes or no. But she did pause at the table to look at the man there.

Putting the suggestion into his head that he needed to find another way of making a living now, she touched her finger to his forehead and let him see what was coming. It was up to him whether he did something about it or not. She heard the woman screaming at him when he got up and left.

"You did save his life, didn't you?" She told him all she'd done was give him information that he could use or not. "And that's all it takes for you to help someone that needs it? Give them something they can do or not?"

"Sometimes it's not so easy as that, but yes, occasionally it does work. If he had stayed, then it would have been his own fault what the outcome would have been." When they were outside of the place she'd been staying, she stood and looked at the nice man. "If I go, you'll heed what I tell you? Everything I say, and so will your family?"

"They'll listen to you. Dylan, she's a bit on the rough side, but she's not afraid of someone having more information than she does and using it." She nodded and looked up and down the street, then back at him. "You gonna tell me what's going on that has you looking over your shoulder so much?"

"They're within ten miles of here. Not my parents, but

11

someone is out there looking for me. I think perhaps it's someone that they contacted." He nodded and told her that they had to get going. "It's not going to do much good—you know that, don't you? They're determined, and they have people that want to explore me. Cut me up and use me in ways that hundreds will die from."

"Together, we can do something that'll keep them away. We, you and I, we're good together, see if we ain't." He laughed then. "Come on then. I noticed that you don't have much to pack up, but we'll get it gathered. I'm telling Dylan and Sunny that we're leaving. You can ride with me in the back. It'll be fun."

She knew that this was a mistake. And though she couldn't see her own future, she knew that they were going to regret her coming back with them. She only hoped that they could forgive her when the time came. Carter knew that they'd be afraid of her too.

~~~

Josh was showing a house when he heard from his grandda that they were coming home. He was glad to hear that, but wasn't able to talk to him right now. The rest of them had plenty to say and to ask, but Grandda just said that he was coming home with two beauties. Only Grandda would think that a woman was a beauty and get away with calling her that to her face.

"Why is it you keep showing us houses that are too small?" He looked at Mr. Riddling and asked him what he meant. "My wife and I want a big house. One we can show off to our families that we got money."

"When you filled out the card, you said that you were downsizing and that you were only looking for a two-bedroom house, with not much in the way of a yard." He handed the man the copy of the search he'd been given. "If you've changed your mind about that, then I'll take care of that right away."

"We only want to live in it for about a month." Josh was confused. "We want them to think that we own it, but we don't want that big. Just for the holidays. And if you could make sure that it has nice furniture in it, that would be great too. We don't have anything that'll fit in a house as big as we want. We want to lord over our parents that we've done so well that they'll be jealous."

"You mean to rent a house that's large? That's furnished as well? I don't think that's going to work. Not to mention, it would be expensive, even if I could find something." Mr. Riddling said if they weren't buying it, they shouldn't have to pay anything for it. "You just want to stay in a lovely home that's completely furnished for a month, as well, as I would assume, the lawns to be completely done. Did you want it decorated too?"

"Yes, that would be really nice. Nothing too elaborate though. We don't do that normally. But it should be ready for us to live in. Food we can bring in for ourselves, I guess." Josh just shook his head at Mrs. Riddling when she spoke. "Also, if you could make sure that there is at least one car, and a limo that we can use while they're here, that would be fantastic as well. Oh yes, and a staff that will do all the cooking and cleaning for us. Just for the month."

"All for you to use for free." Now they looked confused as they assured him that was just what they wanted. "I don't have any kind of service for that. I doubt very much anyone in this line of business does. We're not into renting so much as we're into selling. And as a whole, I don't think anyone in this industry would do the things for you that you've asked me for. If there is nothing else I can help you with, then I'd like to get back to my office."

"Why are you so snippy all of a sudden?" Josh didn't even bother saying anything. "All we wanted to do was to have a little fun in pissing our families off. I don't see why that should make you angry. It's not like you're going to be able to tell them we didn't really buy it. And perhaps we might even throw a little cash your way. You know, like ten or fifteen dollars for helping us out. And your boss told you to make us happy."

"I'm sure she had no idea what you were really wanting, or she wouldn't have set this up for me." Mr. Riddling actually got huffy with him. "If there is nothing else, then I'd really like to go. You've wasted enough of my time."

Josh called his boss as soon as he got them out of the house, which wasn't easy, as they were still trying to convince him that there shouldn't be a problem with this. When he was put on hold, he was sure that the Riddlings had beaten him to it. Not that it mattered to him. He didn't think he'd get fired over this, but if he did, then so be it. Josh was getting sick of people like these two.

Carol was laughing when she came back on the line. "As you might have guessed, I just got a call from Peter and June Riddling. They had quite a story to tell me about you. And I swear to you, Josh, had I known what they were about, I never would have assigned my best agent to them." He said that he knew that. "The nerve of some people. He said you got nasty with him when he mentioned that he didn't think he should have to pay for a house that he was only going to

14

use for a little while. He also said that you promised him a staff, as well as having it furnished. Then you backed out for some reason."

"They had it in their head that I'd not only provide them with this grand house, but have it decorated for the holidays, as well as a limo that they could use. For free, I might add." She said she was sorry. "So am I. Carol, I need to take some time off."

"Whatever you need, Josh, you know that." He did and told her that. "I think you should be thinking about taking over this firm like I spoke to you about a few months ago. I'm too old for this shit too."

"I love working for you. I don't know how I'd be as a boss." She told him he'd be as good at that as he was at whatever he set his mind to. "Maybe, but I need some time to get my head together. And Adam and I are opening this greenhouse, and I'd like to get a good start on that as well."

"But you will come back to me, right?" He said that was his plan, but the more he thought about it, the more he was thinking he'd not go back at all. "Tell me how long you'll need, and I'll put you in for your vacation and such. I think you must have amassed about a month."

"Two, I think. And you don't have to pay me for all of that. Just about a month of it for now. I don't want to hurt you while I'm trying to figure out my life." He saw his grandda coming toward him in the old truck. "Thanks, Carol. If you need me, just call. And if I can help you out I will, but I'm seriously in need of some me time."

When they were together, they hugged as they usually did. He'd been gone longer than he'd thought he would be and was glad to see him. After telling him about his last client, they both had a good laugh about it. Then Grandda turned serious.

"I brought home these two women with us." He asked if Grandma knew. "It ain't like that, you turd head. They're in trouble, and there might be a bit more to it than just saving them. One of them is purely scary in what she can do. Not that she'd hurt me or any of you, but they want her."

"Who does? And you know that we'll help them in any way that we can. But what do you mean, scary with what she can do? You mean kick ass, like Dylan and Sunny?" He said it was magical. "I understand that, Grandda, but that doesn't tell me very much."

"She said that she can kill someone halfway around the world and not leave her chair. That she can lift up cars and throw them should she need to." Josh didn't say anything. He wasn't sure that he believed his grandda; not that he'd lie to him, but the girl might have to him. He asked him if he'd seen her do it. "No. You can't just kill someone like that for a demonstration, now can you? And what do you think would happen if she was to toss a car around like it was nothing but one of them toys that them boys of Evans plays with?"

"Okay, you have a point. But she might be telling you a tale." Grandda just glared at him. "I don't know why you're upset with me—if you believe in her, that's great. But I'll hold out for proof."

"Her momma and daddy are coming to get them. They'll use Rachel to get to Carter. That's their names, Carter and Rachel Compton. Carter is the one that is all powerful. Rachel is a human. She knows a little of what her sister can do, and her parents know some too, but not all, I'm betting." He asked him why they needed them if she had all this power. "Joshua, you're getting on my last bit of nerves. I'm a knight to them, and I want you to help me by being my steed."

"Oh, so I'm to be the horse in all this." Grandda laughed when he did. "Really, what she told you could be a fabrication of a sick mind. Is this the family that Dylan went out there to get? Does she know what's happening with this girl?"

Josh had it in his head that she was just that, a little girl. The other sister was someone that went to school with Dylan, so he knew that she couldn't be very old. And if she was telling his grandda big tales, someone needed to talk to her. He looked at his schedule on his phone and asked him if he could meet this paragon of magic.

"Not if you're going to be nasty about it. She don't need that any more than I do. She's been hurt, Josh. Been in prison for ten whole years for nothing. They let her go because they figured out finally that they had the wrong person. It was the parents all along." He nodded, and then realized that she wasn't a child at all. He asked his grandda how old this girl was. "I think she's about your age. Might be a little younger by a couple of months or so. She was seventeen when they tried her as an adult, due to a cop being killed."

Josh had heard some of this, but he'd been in the middle of shit here and hadn't paid attention. Well, they had his attention now. He talked to Grandda a bit more as they walked to his car. By the time he'd left to go and see about dinner plans with the entire family, Josh had a name and something to go on. No one was going to come here and take advantage of his family. And especially not his grandda.

As soon as he was back to the trailer he was living in until his house was just a little more livable, he pulled out his old computer. Putting in the name Carter Compton, he got a

17

hit right away. He changed while thinking of the news he'd gotten today before sitting down to read about this woman.

In a week, less he was told, he'd be moving into the bedroom, and the kitchen would also be done. The rest, he'd been told, they could work on around him. He was going to take this month off and help his brother in their new partnership, and get his house furnished. He could not wait.

Chapter 2

Rachel just stared at her sister. She wasn't sure that she believed her, or better yet that she wanted to believe her, but she told her most everything. Carter said that she didn't need to know it all at once. The little that she'd told her before was nothing compared to what she'd been told this time. And she was afraid.

"You know that they're coming after me. I know that they said that when you let me listen in to them, but you know that they're actually coming." Carter told her they were nearly there. That's why she was talking to her. "Is this the reason that you didn't want to come here? That you were, I don't know, trying to save me from them?"

"Yes." Carter used to be a lively and funny girl. Dancing all the time when she thought she was alone. And played jokes on anyone that was nearby. She had loved life. Now she was a shell of what she'd been before. "While in prison, I had a lot of time on my hands and I perfected my skills. With skills like mine, there has to be no one around so that they can't tell others what I can do. I'm very good at this, Rachel. I'll keep you as safe as I can."

"You're saying that like you're going to get hurt." She said she didn't know. "You can't see what is going to happen to you?"

"No."

Frustrated, Rachel got up to pace. She was staying with Dylan, but she had no idea where Carter was staying. She said that she'd not be able to handle all the noise and people, and Dylan had told her there was a nice bed and breakfast in town. But when she'd called there to talk to Carter, she was told that she'd never checked in.

"You worry too much. I'm staying in a nice tent that Ollie gave me. And I have blankets and food."

"Don't. Just don't read my mind." She said that she wouldn't unless necessary. "I don't know what constitutes necessary, but this, all this, is a lot to deal with. Why didn't you tell me any of this before? Or were you trying to keep me safe even then?"

"Yes, I'm sorry. But when they get here, and they will sooner or later, you have to be ready for anything."

It was too much to think that their parents would go so far as to kill them both. Which shouldn't surprise her, not with them letting Carter take the fall for what they'd done. Carter looked at the door then, and Rachel did as well. When someone knocked, Carter told her it was Ollie's son.

Opening the door, she saw a younger version of the elderly man she'd spent an enjoyable few days with. After inviting him in, he said he was on a mission from his wife. That he was to bring them home for dinner.

"I've wanted to meet the family, but I'm afraid this—"

Carter told the man that they were going. "Carter, we're not done talking about this. I really think this is important."

"It is. But I have a feeling that they're going to need to know too. But they'll be less believing." Rachel asked her what that meant. "I'll show you what I can do. That'll help the doubts that you have about our parents coming here. But this family—no offense to you—but this family will want more than just the little proof that I can give them, I think."

"I never said I doubted you." Carter touched Rachel's forehead, and she felt the slight buzz from it. "You're reading my mind again. Please don't do that."

"I told you I'd not, and I didn't. But your forehead is wrinkled up like you're thinking too hard. We'll have a nice meal, and then things will be better for you."

She was nearly to the car when she realized that she'd said they'd be better for her, not for them both. Rachel couldn't lose her sister again.

The drive to the house was in a nice limo. She felt sorry for her sister when she crammed herself in the corner of it and didn't say a word. She thought maybe it was because Oliver, what they'd been told to call him, was a large man. Rachel thought it was more than that, but didn't say anything to Carter. She was sort of afraid of what Carter was going to show her. And wondering why she had to wait until they were at the Whitfield home to do it.

As soon as they were at the estate—there was no other name for the plantation styled home, and the pretty rockers on the front with all the flowers—her sister went to the barn and she went into the house with Oliver. There she met some of the boys, as he called them, but two more were due at any moment. They were all very large men, and their wives, those

21

that were married, weren't nearly as big, but were both still the kick assed person she would love to be.

"She'll be all right out there." She looked over at Eve when Rachel went to the window several times. "There are some cows out there, a few horses as well. She'll be just fine. I'm sure that this is a great deal for her to get used to again. All of us in one house is too much for me at times."

"Carter said that she'd show us what she could do. But she was going to do it here." Eve said that they had plenty of land for her to use if it came to that, and no one would be the wiser. "You trust what she's told Ollie to be true?"

"I have no reason to doubt her. Yes, it's hard to believe that anyone would have that much going on, but I'm a woman who turns into a large tiger, so it's easier for me to believe in things that are different. And she is different. I can sense that." Rachel nodded. "I'm going to have one of my boys go out and get her. If you'd like to get cleaned up, we'll be eating soon."

The house was beautiful, and not fake. She had friends that had done their houses to try and mimic this country look, but it was nothing compared to the real thing. This house was homey and warm. There was an air of friendship and love here, something that neither her nor Carter had ever had at home. Then Carter had gone off to prison, and Rachel knew that she hadn't gotten anything there either.

She wanted to cuddle her sister in cotton. Tell her that things were going to be better for them both. But that would be a lie. Things were hard enough on her — they'd be devasting to her sister, she'd bet.

She saw the young man going to the barn, and thought his name was Adrian. He seemed to be the most laid back of all the men, but she'd not met all of them as yet. When he didn't come out of the barn right away, she pulled her coat off the hook and followed him. She was afraid for them both.

The barn was just what she'd thought it would be on a ranch like this. There were several stalls that had horses in them, and one or two that had cows. As soon as she heard Carter talking to the other man, she knew that her fears were unfounded, that he was just talking to her about the cattle.

"Mary here is about due to have herself another baby." Carter didn't speak, or if she did it was too low for her to hear. "Yes, that's right, in a week. This is her fourth delivery, and sadly the last. She's getting too old for walking around and carrying the extra weight."

"Carter." She looked up from the stall when she came around the corner. "I thought you were coming in to eat. They're waiting on us."

"I know." She looked at the man again. "She's not too old. But she thinks that you're taking her away from here and she'll not return. Mary knows that has happened to some of the other cattle you have here."

"You can talk to her?" Carter told him they could all talk if they wanted to listen. "I don't know what to say."

"Come on, let's go in."

They were headed to the door when Adrian called her back. Carter just turned and looked at him when he asked her if it was a boy or girl.

"Both."

Then she walked away, and Adrian stood there for several seconds before he began to follow. It was comical, Rachel thought, that she was having so much trouble wrapping her head around her sister's abilities, when this man just took it for gospel what she'd told him.

Carter was hanging up her coat in the mud room when they entered. She didn't go into the warm kitchen right away, but stood back and let them all greet her. Rachel knew that it was because of how many men there were in the kitchen and that she was frightened, but before she could explain, Eve took the men to task and made them each carry in a platter or bowl of food to the dining room. When they were the only three in the room, she asked her sister if she was all right.

"Yes. Why wouldn't I be? They're large men, and I suppose I have to get used to seeing people in crowds."

Eve said that she'd take care that they behaved at the table, and Carter nodded. Rachel went to the table with a platter of pork chops, and Carter was given two baskets of hot rolls. Eve came in behind her with a second bowl of baked potatoes.

Rachel was seated between two of the men—Evan, who was married to Dylan, and David, who was married to Sunny. They were both very polite, and she didn't mind being put between them. Carter stood by the wall, not moving until Ollie came to help her.

"Come on, darling, you can sit here with me." She nodded and looked at him. But Rachel noticed that he didn't touch her as she might have. "These are my grandsons, the ones I was telling you about."

One of them stood up and sat down twice before he finally stayed put. It was the strangest thing when Dylan started laughing with Evan. Then everyone at the table did. Carter shied away from them, but Ollie asked her not to leave. The man, she thought his name was Josh, stood up again, and this time went to stand by her sister.

"I won't touch you." Carter looked at Rachel, panic in her eyes. "I promise you, I won't touch you without your consent. But I'm going to sniff your neck if you don't mind."

"Please, don't touch me." He promised her again that he'd not. And then he leaned in and sniffed her neck. Carter shivered, and the man stood there, stiff. Something had happened in that moment, and she wasn't sure what it was. "You don't want me. I'm not right."

"We'll work this out." Carter looked at Rachel when she said her name. But the man answered. "She's my mate. Carter is my mate, and neither of us are prepared for it, I think."

"I'm not right." He asked Carter what she might mean by that. Instead of answering him, she moved to the door that led out to the decking around the house. He followed, and a few seconds later, the rest of them did as well. "Watch. This is why my parents are coming for me. And if you'll trust me not to hurt anything or anyone, then I can give you an idea of my abilities."

Carter didn't move. Didn't lift her hands up to the sky as she'd seen done on television when people were summoning their magic. She had no idea what she expected, but when the truck that two of the men had arrived in settled next to her on the lawn, no one moved or said a word.

The tree in the yard shook hard. The car was set on its nose, then the bed. As it was doing its dance, the fence, old and sagging, was popped from the ground and rolled up. In seconds there was new fencing there. New poles were slammed into the ground as the fencing curved its way along the wooden stakes in a straight line. Carter never moved, never took her eyes off the people surrounding her on the deck. And when the truck made its way to the front again,

Josh joined her in the yard.

"What can I do for you? Are you weak? Do you need something to replenish yourself?" Carter asked him if he'd seen what she'd done. "I did. It was impressive, if you don't mind me saying so. But that had to be draining on you. What do you need?"

"Nothing. I don't think you understand. I can do a great deal more than that." He grinned, and even from where Rachel stood, she could see that Carter was upset with him. "You have to be terrified. I'm a freak of nature."

"Listen to me, all right?" Carter nodded. "I want you to look there on the deck. At the people standing there. Do any of them look frightened? Do they look disgusted by what you just did?" Her sister did look at the people there, she did as well, and noticed that they all were smiling.

"No." Carter seemed to be stiffer rather than relaxed at that. Then she looked at the people on the deck. "Go into the house. Now."

No one hesitated even for a second. Dylan went to stand with them, Josh standing between the two women. Even from her vantage point from the dining room, she could see that Dylan was talking to her. What was being said, she didn't know, but when the man came out of the woods with his hands up, no one moved.

~~~

Josh wasn't sure who he was, but he wasn't moving any closer to them. When Dylan asked if either one of them knew him, before he could say no, Carter started talking. He felt his heartrate double. He was working with the man who had come to his home earlier in the week.

"He's a scout, looking for property that is off the beaten

26

path and has a great many trees. He goes by the name of Charlie Bloom, and he works for a man by the name of Moody. Thomas Langley is another man that works with his boss. The boss is Waldo Moody." Dylan said that she knew the name. "He's also a hunter, big game he calls it. But it's really humans that he finds and puts out in the property for several days with food and water. Then when he has enough people that have paid him, they go hunting for the person. And kill him."

"Any shifters?" Carter told him that was their next big game. "I don't think so. I'm going to ask my brother to call the police. Do you know where Moody is?"

"No. I can find him, but I don't have him as yet." Josh looked at Carter when she said his name. "He knows that you own a half-done house, and he's going to take advantage of that and burn you out. That's what he was going to do today, but was lost for some time before stumbling across the pack."

"Mother fuck."

He went to the deck and spoke to Evan. The house needed to be done now, not in a few weeks from now. Evan said he'd call in some favors and get it done. Carter stayed where she was, and that was when it occurred to him that she was holding the man somehow. He made his way back to her. "Are you hurting him? Please don't. The police will need to talk to him, and I'd rather he was in jail then have to explain his death to them. Besides, the paperwork is hard to get filled out."

"He'll be right here until they come for him." Dylan asked her how she was doing that. "He believes himself to be chained there and cannot move. While we know better, he sees the chains wrapped around his arms and legs as if they

27

are there. No matter what he does, he cannot break them to move."

Josh laughed. It really wasn't all that funny, but Carter wasn't doing anything other than fucking with the man's mind. He asked her if she'd gotten her information from him, and could she make him tell the police the truth.

"He will."

When she walked to the front of the house, he started to follow her when Grandda beat him to it. He knew that they were close and that Grandda really liked her, but he wasn't sure what to do now. She was his mate, yes, but she was stronger than anything he'd ever encountered.

Adrian moved close to him to speak quietly. "Josh, she knew he was coming and warned us. Then she made him think he was in trouble and couldn't move. That's one hell of a mind that she has there." He nodded, still trying to wrap his mind around the fact that she'd lifted a truck like it was nothing at all. "Can you imagine what someone could do with her if she fell into the wrong hands? We need to keep her safe, and Rachel too. I have a feeling that if Rachel were hurt, all bets would be off on Carter using everything that she has."

The police arrived about five minutes later. No sooner than they walked toward the man, he was telling them why he'd been in the woods, what his plan had been about Josh's house, and that he'd had a gun, but a wolf had taken it.

Josh went to find Carter. She was sitting on the porch steps. Grandda was in the rocker, and when he saw him, Grandda waved at him, telling him he was going to clean up for dinner, and left them there. Sitting next to her but far enough away so that he'd not brush against her just yet, he looked to where she was looking and saw the two wolves standing there, as if on guard.

"My parents are coming here. They're going to take...they were going to take Rachel to try and bring me in line to go with them. They've sold me to somebody at a lab that wants to study me. But there are others too. A man in the Army wants me for himself to use as a weapon." He asked her if she knew names. "I do. They don't know about the other. My parents have sold me to three different people for just over three million dollars. However, they're broke."

"You said that they were going to take your sister. I'm assuming that something has changed, and they no longer take her." She said it was him. "I save her? Or my family does?"

"They take you, I think. Their names are Lee and Hazel Compton. They'll be responsible for several deaths before getting here. I can't stop them from killing them. I've learned that if I intercede, the person dies anyway. The only thing I can do is give the victims information that they can heed or not. Most of the time, in my experience, they don't. I'm going to kill them, both my parents, I hope. Before they get to anyone here." He asked her if she could see her own future. "No, and not yours either. I can see my sister's now, and they no longer take her. I'm assuming, and probably correctly so, that they'll take you, as I said. I can see the rest of your family, but not ours. I can't be your mate, Josh. You have to know that I'm not right."

"You keep saying that, but I don't understand it any more than I did the first time you said it. Perhaps you can tell me why you can do this. Did someone do this to you, or were you born with these abilities? And I know that you were in prison, but I'm thinking that you could have left at any time you wished."

"I did, several times, but I always came back. I needed to protect my sister, and sometimes I'd have to be there to do so." He nodded, sure that there was more to it than her just helping her sister. "I was born this way. When I was just a kid, I would bring myself food and some for Rachel. She never knew, of course, but I tried very hard to keep us from being hurt too much by our parents. Then when she moved out, I thought she'd be safe for a while, that I could move out as well. But Mom caught me moving something, and after that, it wasn't an easy life for me. They had me helping them on all manner of things. Stealing things like food when they wanted it. The newspapers too. Never anything big, because they didn't have any idea how strong I'd gotten. In prison, I practiced until I was where I am now. I was in prison because of them. They robbed the bank. I had nothing to do with it, you have to believe me on that. I'd been celebrating my birthday when I was arrested. And when they disappeared, I was blamed for the entire thing, even though I hadn't been near the bank."

"Then why did they think that you did this?" She lifted her hand up, and he watched as things, shapes he couldn't make out, danced there. When he saw her parents in what he assumed was the bank, they were dropping hair from a brush and leaving behind some of her clothing. "So they made it look as if you had robbed the bank by doing that. Your parents are bastards; you know this, don't you?"

"Yes." She stood up and so did he. While she walked around, looking at the yard, he tried to think of what he could do to help her. Nothing, came to his mind. She was just what the Army wanted her for, a weapon. "You can understand

30

now, can't you? Why this won't work for us."

"No, I don't. We'll have some things to work out between us. Like this no touching rule that you have." He was going for humor, but he thought it was lost on her. "I'm a very patient man, Carter. And I'm going to do everything I can to help you with this. I might not have wanted a mate right now, but you're here, and I'm going to help you in any way that I can so that you don't get hurt either."

"I could kill you." He said that she could and asked her if she wanted to. "No. You have a good heart, and nothing untoward in your head. You're sick of your job, but you've taken care that you can have some time to yourself. If we come together, and I'm not saying that we should, you'll have to make adjustments to your life. And I know that you aren't that easy to have change in your life."

"No, not usually. But this is important. To us both." She turned and looked at him. "I would like nothing more than to touch you. Your skin looks to be so soft and inviting. But I don't want to hurt you in anyway. I'm not even sure why you don't want someone to touch you."

"I can get all that you have in your mind. Things that you more than likely don't want me to know." He touched his fingers to her cheek and she closed her eyes. "It's been so long since anyone touched me. I've missed it more than I thought I would. I kept telling myself I was better off, but this, this feels like heaven to me. I beg of you, don't let me go just yet, please?"

"I won't." Josh wanted to kiss her, but he didn't. His cat seemed to be content with just touching her this way as well. And when she looked at him, Josh pulled her into his arms and held her against his body. It was the best sensation that

31

he'd ever had. "You're very warm. Warmer than I thought for this time of year. And you're too thin. I would imagine that I'd be as well had I only prison food to eat."

He was babbling, but didn't care. He was holding her, and that made him and his cat content for now. She was wounded, their mate, and they both knew that anything that they did or said right now would set the tone for their relationship. When she pulled back and looked up at him, he stared into her clear blue eyes and saw her fear mirrored back at him. He was afraid for her, not of her.

"No one will hurt you." She nodded, but didn't say anything as he continued. "I might get hurt, but it'll be to try and keep you safe. And your sister. Though I think she's a good deal stronger than she lets on. And you're very strong. But I'll be there for both of you, forever now."

"If you do, then you'll die." He nodded, and started to tell her so long as she was safe it mattered little to him. But Evan came around the corner of the house and asked if they were hungry.

"We're coming. Thanks." He didn't let her go just yet but did ask her if she was sure about that. That he would die if they stayed together. She told him that she wasn't sure of anything concerning him. "Then we'll cross that bridge when we get to it. Until then, I'll try to learn that you're stronger than me, and more than likely able to take on someone that I'd not be able to handle. As a tiger, that's the best I can give you for now. We're a manly sort of being, and I'm not sure how good I'll be at stepping out of your way. But I will try. For you."

Josh held her hand as they made their way back to the dining room. He was also glad to see that someone had adjusted the plates and chairs around so that she could sit next to him. Nothing was clear to him yet, what was happening, what else she could do, but he knew one thing for sure—he was thrilled to death to have her there. Despite what he had said to his brother.

Everyone spoke more quietly than they normally did. There was still a lot of shouting and talking over each other, but she ate, and that was important too. Josh knew that he had his work cut out for him with her. And then there was the added problems of Langley coming, as well as Carter's parents. But one day at a time, one issue at a time too. He just hoped that he got his house finished before anyone else came around to burn it down. Otherwise the two of them would be spending the rest of their lives in the camper that his parents had loaned him.

Chapter 3

Waldo Moody, otherwise known as Sheppard to the people of the town he'd been about to buy out, wasn't happy with the way things were going. First of all, two of his hunters had backed out of the last hunt and had demanded their money back. He'd not forked it over, of course. All deals were final, he told them. And now they were threatening him with exposure. Like that was going to bother him. No one knew anything about him, and that's the way he liked it.

"Bloom has been arrested. And from what I've heard, he's telling them whatever they want to know. Even things that I'm sure that they don't ask. I've tried to get in to see him, but that's a no go. He admitted to trying to burn out the other property you wanted, and now they'll be all over that." Waldo asked Tommy where he was. "Your favorite little town. Apparently, he'd been caught snooping around some of that property that you wanted and got caught. I'm not sure how they managed it, but he's now sitting in their jail, and has lawyered up with some public defender."

"He has to go. Take care of that." Tommy told him that he had a man on it now. "Good. Any more news on that land out there with the house on it? I'm telling you, that's is exactly what I've been looking for. Flat enough that they can see the prey, and there are enough trees on it so that the little bastards can hide out too. Perfect. When did that guy buy it up?"

"He didn't. The land belongs to his parents, who gifted it to him about a year ago. He's been working on the house since then. It's state of the art too, from what I could find out about it. He's living in a camper next to the house until he can move in." Waldo asked him what he was going to do about that. "Again, I have someone on it. You should know that the Whitfields are a big name around these parts. Just to hear someone talk about them, you'd swear that they must walk on water. And they're very rich."

"How rich? As a whole, just what am I up against here? And what's it going to take to get him off my land?" He told him the figure that he'd been able to get. "Christ, that's a fucking ton of money. And you said something about one of them that carries a weapon. Do you know why she is? I mean, is she a dyke or something?"

"No, not that I've heard. She is married to one of the Whitfields. They have a couple of kids. Teenagers that I couldn't get to even if I wanted." Waldo asked him why not. "They're guarded better than anyone that I've been up against. And they don't any of them have a set schedule either. It's like they know that we're trying to get to them and are being covert. I'd say someone had training in that, but none of the men have served in any armed forces. This woman has something to do with it, but I've not been able to find out much about her other than she's a rule breaker. Not the kind of person that I like to go up against without plenty of fire power."

"Adrian Whitfield—I saw some posters about him running for office. Do we think he could use some extra votes that we can provide for him? Give him an edge that the other man doesn't have?" Tommy told him what he knew. "That's not possible. You mean to tell me that he's running unopposed, because he's doing such a good job that no one wants to run against him?"

"That's what I heard. He's really this nice sap. Helped get the schools back in order when the last mayor hadn't. He and his family run all kinds of things in town, own most of it as well. The one you want, Joshua? He just took a leave of absence from his job to get his home in order. They're clean, not a single skeleton in any of their closets." Waldo asked about the women. "Sunshine Whitfield. She's a big-time reporter that does some of that exposé shit that you hate. Where she goes in and gets dirt on the person running a less than legal operation. Then she goes to the newspaper and runs this tell all. It runs in more than the local too—she's international. An independent that gets her man, so they say. And on her last job she exposed all kinds of shit going down that was supposed to have gotten her nearly killed. They bounce back better than a fucking cat would."

"What about the other one; what can you tell me about her? Other than she's this woman that carries and you're afraid of her." He said nothing. "There has to be something. Does she work? Is there any bad credit on her record?"

"I don't know. I kid you not, Waldo, she's just gone off the rails or something. If I'd have not seen her, I'd swear that she wasn't a real person. There was a report about her from a while back, how she was this war hero or something like that. Then nothing. Not anything about having those kids or what she's doing. There isn't a record of her ever having a driver's license, a bank account, or even a fucking library card. She doesn't exist, as far as I can find out."

"What is it about this family that makes it so damned difficult to get one of them to deal with me? I tried to be nice about this, and they didn't want that. What is it about them that makes them untouchable?" Tommy said he was still digging, but so far nothing. "If you can't find anything, then make it up. I can run a smear campaign as easily as I can anything else. And this might hurt their boy running for office so much that they'll know I mean business."

"I'll get on that." Tommy was headed out the door when he called him back. When he was seated again, Waldo asked him about the next hunting trip. "We've had those two back out, and they're making a stink, so you know. But this morning when I checked the reservations, two more have quit us. Neither of them gave a reason, and neither of them asked for a refund. I have a feeling this is going to get worse before it gets better. You might not need the land if this keeps up."

When he left, Waldo pulled out the map of the area that he'd had printed at the bursar's office. He wished now that he'd paid the extra money to get the one with the names on them. It would have made things slightly better for him in looking them up. He looked at the land that he had a pending sale on and was just thinking about the small ten-acre plot when his phone rang. Picking it up, he just said hello but nothing more.

"The bid that you have on the land out on Forty has been declined." Waldo asked him what had happened. "Well, you knew it was going to the highest bidder — we needed it off the books. So that's what we did, took the highest bidder. You weren't even in the same ball park."

"Can you tell me who won the bid? Perhaps I can persuade them to sell it to me for a profit." The man told him he doubted that the winner would sell. "And why not? Who doesn't like to make a little extra in a deal like this?"

"The Whitfields purchased it because it butted up against their land. They own quite a bit of it too. I'm thinking that they'll not sell it because of that. You can try, but I'm telling you right now, they probably won't take you up on your offer." Waldo asked which one bought it. "They all did. That's how they do business. They buy it as a family, then when one of them wants it or they have to build on it, whoever needs it just gets it given to them. They're a good family. Not just to each other, but to everyone they encounter. Until you piss them off — then all bets are off with them. You'll likely never know what hit you when they come after you."

They were quickly becoming a pain in his ass was what they were. When he hung up with the man, he sat there in his chair thinking about the shit that was going on right now. The fact that he was losing hunters didn't bother him overly much. He could keep the money, and did, but they'd never be able to hunt with him again. But there was too much going on right now to not think that something was going on behind the scenes. Just what, he had no idea. But he'd find out, and soon too.

It took him nearly two hours of calling in favors to get something on any of them, and it had been for nothing. Not only did he not have the people in his pocket for something that they'd done, but he also had nothing at all to show for his work. His favors were now lost to him, and he was no closer to finding out about the Whitfields than he had been before. Not even maiden names for the women.

Waldo looked at his scribbled notes and wondered who was working against him in this. There had to be someone higher than him on the food chain. Perhaps one of the men who had backed out was trying to get himself a hunting group together. As he began searching for their names and shit on them, he found himself staring at the one picture that he'd been able to find.

It was of the men with their parents, the article said. They were big mother fuckers, each of them at least six and a half feet tall, and he'd bet that every one of them worked out by lifting tires from tractors as fun. That's what he'd heard that these people from the sticks did—roll a tractor tire to build up muscles. For all he knew they could be rolling tractors, they were that big. But the picture did him no good, because all it said was they were the Whitfield family and that they were out for an evening of fun.

On his way home later that night, he stopped by his favorite deli and ordered himself a pastrami sandwich on rye, as well as a nice thick roast beef for Tommy. They'd fortify themselves with dinner before looking over anything that they could find about these people. And the ones that had backed out from the hunt. He didn't know why, but he thought that something was going on there. He'd just have to figure it out and take care of it.

At midnight he went to bed. Tommy hadn't shown up, nor had he called. Waldo had thought about calling him, just to get an update on things, but Tommy's phone went to voice mail right away instead of just ringing. Waldo wasn't in the habit of leaving messages, and he wasn't going to start now, no matter how pissed off he was. Knowing that Tommy would be calling him soon and would hear Waldo rant at him for an hour at least, Waldo took his cell up to his room with him, just in case.

At two ten his phone started ringing. It took him a long time to realize it was his phone and not the alarm clock that he was trying to turn off. When he finally answered, he barked at the person that it had better be important when he heard the heavy breathing. Before he could stop the adrenaline rushing over his skin, Tommy started talking quickly and quietly to him.

"You need to let it go. The property, the hunting, all of it, let it go." There was a loud scream, but he wasn't sure who it was from. He'd never known Tommy to scream before. "Don't go after the Whitfields, Waldo. They're dangerous." Then the line went dead.

Waldo wasn't sure that he knew what was going on, but the fact that Tommy had been hurt bothered him a bit. The kid had been working for him for a long time, and he didn't like that he might be out there suffering. Not that he'd go find him...no, never that, but he was worried about how much he might have told whoever warned him off about the Whitfields.

At three-thirty he was still awake and thinking about Tommy when he got up. There wasn't any point in lying in a bed with shit that he had to do. Just as he pulled on his robe and made his way down the stairs, there was a thump at the front door, then the screech of tires. He told his butler to see what it was, but to be careful.

The door opened slowly, and when Patterson staggered

back, he went to the door to see what it was. Waldo wasn't sure that he wanted to see whatever it was that made the other man, a stout man that seemed to let nothing bother him, lean against the wall as pale as a silk sheet.

There on the steps to the front of his house was Tommy, and he'd been beaten up pretty badly. Telling Patterson to call the police, he felt for his pulse and felt the bones in his neck instead. Tommy's throat had been cut all the way to his spine, and he was nearly sick on his body before staggering back as well.

"Sir, he'd dead." He wanted to tell him that he could see that, but he was fighting hard with his belly. "I've called the police. They'll be here soon."

There was no way that a man had done this to him. Not a human anyway. This was the work of a vampire, and he'd find out who too. He had friends that would rat out their own mother for the right amount of money, and his vampire friend would do the same. Hell, he had done the same. But he had pissed the vampire off once too often, and he'd told him he'd never help again.

"Before they get here, call Randolph. Tell him I have a dead man here that I think a vampire killed. Tell him to hurry, that I didn't think about it before they were called. Beg him if you have to."

Patterson said he'd do so now and pulled out his cell. "Shall I tell him the usual?"

"Yes, whatever he wants, I need to know who killed Tommy."

When Randolph showed up seconds after Patterson hung up the phone, he didn't speak but went straight to the body and sniffed him. When he backed away from him, Waldo asked him if he could find them.

"Yes, but I won't." He asked him why the fuck not. "Because this is a vampire that you do not wish to have as an enemy. And I won't risk him killing me. Because once I start looking for him, I might as well meet the sun. He's a good friend, and a worse enemy. He's not one that I'd mess with on my best day."

"I'll pay you whatever you want. With that, you should be able to hide from him." Randolph said that he'd never be able to hide from this particular vampire. "What the hell does that mean? I want him dead for killing Tommy."

"Then you will have to do it on your own. I will not try and come up against this vampire. He's stronger than any other one I know, and it is said that he has the help of a fae." He didn't know what that meant, but didn't ask. "As of now, I'll do no more work for you. If you have him after you, I am finished. As I have said to you before this, do not call me again, Waldo. Our relationship is over."

With that said, Randolph disappeared. There wasn't time for him to call the man back; the police showed up with guns drawn. He wondered what they'd do if he told them that a vampire had killed his friend. More than likely laugh in his face.

Waldo went to his office after answering all their questions a dozen times. Then when the body was taken away, they stuck around for another hour before they seemed satisfied that he'd not killed Tommy.

It was nearly eight in the morning when he was getting out of the shower to finish up his work for the day. The police had gone some time ago, telling him that they'd look into Tommy's death right away. There would be no looking into it, even he knew that.

Now he had to find the vampire that killed Tommy, something else to add to his list of shit to do. He wondered where he could find this so called scary vampire and his fae. He'd have to put out feelers, he thought, and hope someone knew who he was. Waldo wanted him dead, and right now.

"And I'll see to it that he is, too. I'm not afraid of a vampire. I'll show him that when I find him."

He wasn't going to be able to get any help with it until tonight, but he had a list of people he was going to call. Then he was going to deal with the Whitfields; they'd been a pain in his ass long enough.

~~~

Carter got up and took a shower. Old habits, she knew, would be hard to break. After getting her shower, she made her bed then sat in one of the many chairs in the room that she'd been given. The house was coming along nicely, and she was glad that he was getting it finished. When someone knocked on the door, she bid them enter and was surprised by the tiny fae that came in the room from under the door.

"My name is Flora. I work with Tanner—he's a powerful vampire." Carter nodded, not sure what this had to do with her. "I have a piece of cloth for you to touch for him. Please, you may say no if you wish, but he has asked this favor of you, and he will owe you a great boon."

"Why does he want me to touch it and not Sunny? It's my understanding that she can touch things and find people as well." Flora said that he'd only asked her to bring it to her. "And why does he want the information I'll get from this? Is he going to kill this person?"

"He is dead already. But he wishes to see if you can tell

him what else is going on with his boss. He wishes his real name." Carter looked at the stained cloth and realized that it was blood. "This man, he was coming after my friend, the vampire, and he had to stop him. It was only then that he figured out what his plan was concerning our friends the Whitfields. There is another, someone that he works for, that he'd like to take care of as well."

"His name is Waldo Moody. The dead man was Tommy Langley." She asked how she was getting that without touching the cloth. "Because I don't need it when there is blood. I only need to smell it and it comes to me. Why did he kill him in such a way, then dump him on the doorstep of this Moody? Wouldn't it have served him better to turn the man over to him to get more information?"

"Nay, it would not." She looked at the large vampire standing in the doorway. "May I enter? I don't need your permission, but I would like to have it. You are very timid, and I don't wish to frighten you any more than you've been."

"I've had some rough times of it." He said that he understood better than she would know. "You lost someone recently. Your lover and mate. He died saving another from the slaughter that was happening around him. He was a good man."

"Thank you for that. Can you tell me if he suffered much?" Carter told him that he'd not suffered at all. He was dead long before the sun was let in to dispose of the bodies. "Again, I thank you for the information. I had no way of knowing since he was blocked from me. It will ease my heart a great deal now that I know that he didn't suffer needlessly."

"Why is it important to you that you know who this other man is?"

He sat in the chair across from her and said nothing. They were still staring at each other when Josh came into the room. It was then that she realized that Tanner had called to Josh, so that he'd be able to speak to her freely.

"This man wishes to kill off humans on the land that is here now." Carter nodded—she knew that already. "I don't want any more of my kind, nor my friends, to be harmed in this. The Whitfields are very good to me. And that would include you, my dear."

"You were told what I can do, weren't you?" Tanner said that he'd heard some of it, but not all. "I can hurt you. Kill you too, no matter what you have done to enhance your body. I don't have any reason to; as you said, you're only helping this family out. If I asked you to step away from this, that I have it covered, would you?"

"Do you?" She nodded at him. "This man, he'll pay for what he's done to others? He'll pay dearly? His boy tried to kill me the other night. He came at me for no other reason than that he could. His death meant nothing to me until I realized what his purpose was in being out so late at night. He wants to find dirt on this family."

"Moody, I promise you, will pay with his life. But not today. And there will be no more deaths of the innocent by his hand. I have taken care that there will be no more hunts." Tanner touched her mind and she let him. There wasn't anything in her head that she'd hide from anyone so long as they weren't trying to hurt her. "Have you seen enough?"

"You are still wounded by what was done to you in there. I should like for you to tell your mate what has been done so that he can better understand what you've endured. He and his family can help you." Carter said that she didn't need any help, but thanked him. "If you do not tell him, then I will have to. There isn't any reason for you to suffer through this alone."

"I am alone. And that's the way it should be." Tanner looked at Josh, but she stared at the vampire. "Will you leave Moody alone? For now? I will tell you when it's time, should you wish, but I'll kill him."

"I will await your call. But if one more innocent dies by his hand, then I will come for him. The man must pay for what he's done." She told him that she'd allow it then. "And you'll tell Josh what you have been made to do? Today?"

"He'll hate me." Tanner stood up and touched his fingers to her cheek. His hands were surprisingly warm, and she found herself wanting to curl into that warmth, and she knew what he was doing. "You've given me some of your magic. Why would you do that? I don't need any more."

"I have given you the ability to allow him to see what I have. The whole of it." She looked at Josh then, and wondered what he'd think of her when he knew. "He will continue to love you, dear child. And he will help you with this. There is no better man nor family that you can depend on."

After Tanner left them with the promise of waiting for her to call, she looked at Josh. He was dressed as he had been yesterday, in jeans and a T-shirt. Carter looked around the room and wondered what it would be like to have something so wonderful as a home like this. But she knew that if she didn't tell him what Tanner had seen, then he would.

"They knew what I was in prison. Not all, but enough that they used me for things. One of the many things that I was forced to do was stand at the entrance every shift that the guards had and touch the inmates. All of them. And then

47

I was to tell the guards what they'd been up to, what they'd done that day, and if any of them had bribed anyone or had been having sex with other inmates." He said that they had used her as a snitch. "Something like that at the start. Then after a time they used me for other stuff, like the races. Lottery winnings, as well as telling them when they were to have a surprise inspection or something similar. They forced me to do these things or they'd take me to the laundry room and tie me up."

"They'd rape you." She shook her head and he didn't understand, she could see that. "Tell me, love, what did they do to you that made you cooperate with them? I'm sure that it was horrific for you."

"They would tie me up and have all the inmates that were on death row touch me while thinking of what they'd done to their victims. There was one particular woman who had murdered several children. I would see what she did to them, how she had eaten parts of them. She thought that it would make her younger by eating any part of them. When it didn't work, she would blame it on the child and go after another, then another, until she was caught." She watched his face. "I had no choice in the matter. It was that or I would go insane from all the sights and sounds I would hear when they were touching me. And even when they locked me up in the pit, it wasn't nearly as bad as reliving the death of all those people over and over."

She took his hands into hers and guided them slowly to her head. He could have pulled away should he have wanted to, but he let her take his hands there so that he could see what she had. As soon as his hands were on her head, she closed her eyes and let him inside of her mind. Carter knew the exact moment that he saw what she did.

Carter hadn't meant to kill the guard and they all knew it. But it didn't save her from being tortured for several weeks. For them to teach her a lesson that she'd never forgotten. But the guard was killing one of the inmates by strangulation, and she stopped him with all the power that she could, smashing his body against the wall until he was nothing more than a pile of uniform and blood.

When he saw all that she had, his hands moved away from her. Carter didn't love him. She wasn't even sure that she liked him very much. He'd not been mean or anything to her, but she knew that his rejection would cut her to her very soul.

"How long did this go on? How long did they have you tied up with these people before you were released?" She told him. "Every week while you were in prison, they took you down there and made you see that. Why? If you were helping them, why did they not stop it? And this man that you had to kill—and it was justified as far as I'm concerned—what happened to his body after he was killed?"

"He was buried on the land adjacent to the prison. But the other, they needed to keep me in line. In case I wasn't telling them everything that they wanted to know." Josh stood, and she put her hands in her lap as he walked toward the fireplace in the room, taking a bit of her heart with him. "At some point in my stay there, someone decided that I could travel to the men's prison as well. There I was subjected to much worse images and sounds. This went on for months. I'd be tied in the sublevels, made to endure what they did, then taken to the men's prison for a few hours of that. It was never ending."

"Does anyone else know about this?" She said that she'd

49

never told anyone. She was ashamed. "Why are you ashamed that they tortured you and hurt you? My God, I want to go there and kill every one of them. And I will too."

"You don't have to say that." He looked at her from his position at the fireplace. "I can go and stay with my sister now. I've not told her, so she'll be all right with me—"

"Don't leave me." She looked at him as he sat in front of her, taking her hands into his. His touch was gentle, belying the anger and turmoil that she could see in his face. "They are going to pay for this. And I'm not sure why you thought that leaving here was something that I'd want, but I don't. You were a victim. As much as the ones that you had to watch every day."

"I might not ever be any different than I am now. Afraid to be touched, terrified that I'll do something wrong and end up back in prison, forever this time. I'm not the same person I was ten years ago. I don't know if I ever will be again." Josh kissed her on the mouth, and then looked at her. "You should be careful, Josh. I know that your kind loves fast and hard. You don't want to fall in love with me."

"I've already fallen in love with you. The moment that you told my family to hide when that man came to the house, I knew then that I'd love you if you'd allow it. I know now that you didn't just suffer at the hands of your parents, but the people who were paid to keep you safe while you were there." He kissed her again, gently, like she was a small child that he didn't want to scare. "I'm in love with you, Carter. I would do anything for you. Would kill for you if need be. These people, they'll be dealt with, and dealt with now. I won't do it, for I think you'd see that. But I can make a few calls, and it'll be over for them and anyone else that is at their mercy."

"I don't understand you. You or your family." He put his forehead onto hers and laughed. "I think you all need your heads examined. This isn't what I expected."

"Good. It's nice that I can keep you on your toes. You certainly have me since I met you." Laughing, he stood up again, pulling her up from the chair. "I'm starving, and I know that we've not hired anyone to cook for us so we'll have to wing it. Can you cook?"

"No. I never got to learn how." He said that he could make eggs and bacon, as well as pancakes. "I love pancakes."

"Then pancakes it is. Hopefully there is enough stuff down there to make them. I've brought all my supplies from the camper and stocked the kitchen. Oh, you might be surprised to find that a lot more of the house is done. By the end of the week, we'll be having furniture delivered. After we go pick it out." He took her hand and led her down the stairs to the kitchen. "We also need to get you some clothes. I want to see you in something bright and pretty, as beautiful as you are."

When she was sitting in the chair in the kitchen, all she could think about was that he was in love with her. And that he didn't care what had happened to her. She wondered if he would some night when she was having a nightmare about it. For now he'd not know the haunts that she had, and she could hide them from him. But if he slept with her, there wouldn't be any way that he'd not know that she woke in terror nightly. She'd cross that bridge when she got to it. No point in borrowing trouble, her sister was always saying. Perhaps he'd not want to sleep with her. There was always that.

Chapter 4

Josh closed up his computer when he finished reading the article. There really wasn't that much out there on telekinesis, and some of it he wasn't so sure was right. He lived with someone that could and did use it, and some of those people that wrote the articles that he read no more understood it than he did. When Carter joined him in the office, he smiled at her. He loved what she was wearing.

"I'm not sure this is me." He asked her why not. "I don't know. I'm not a big flower type of person. It's very bright, isn't it?"

"It is, and it makes your eyes shine. I also love what you did with your hair. The braid is much easier than all of it hanging down in your eyes all the time." She fingered the braid and looked around the office. "What do you think of this room? I got most of the furniture for it at the second-hand shop in town. But I'm not sure about the chair. It's not very comfortable for long periods of time."

"If you want to know something, you can just ask me."

He asked her what she meant. "You want me to tell you about the pieces, correct?"

"No. If that was what I wanted, I would have asked. But I was only making conversation about the room to put you at ease. You seem to be very tense today." She nodded. "What is it, Carter? Did something happen?"

"I have nightmares." He told her that he knew that. "I woke you last night. I'm sorry. Sometimes I can catch the screams, but other times, like last night, I can't."

"What is it you dream about?" She looked out the window, and he could tell that she was nervous or afraid to tell him. "I used to have nightmares when I was a kid. Not like, I'm sure, you have, but I was afraid of the dark. Like terrified. I'd gotten accidently locked in the basement once, and that was all it took."

"I hear them. Other people's dreams and thoughts. It's harder to shut out when I'm asleep. They come to me, and I can see what they're thinking. What they plan to do." He didn't say anything; this was well beyond what he had read about today. "One of your neighbors is planning his death. He is very ill, and feels as if he can't go on. His name is Rogers."

He wrote the name down to tell Evan, so he could maybe talk to him. "Carter, come here. I'd very much like to hold you. If it doesn't hurt you."

"It doesn't when you touch me. It usually makes me feel all sorts of things that you're doing, but yesterday, I noticed that there was only a feeling of comfort. That's what I want to talk to you about." He didn't move, thinking that they could be progressing to something bigger. "Will you sleep with me? Before it gets too far along. Us, I mean."

"I don't know what that means, but if you're referring

to us falling in love, it's much too late for that. I'm in love with you. I told you that last night." She nodded, and he saw the tears then. "Don't cry, love. I'm sorry that you're going through this, and I don't know how to help you."

"I need a rock. A lifeline I can hold on to when it gets bad. When someone touches me that has thoughts, I need someone, I think, to hold me down, to keep me centered." She looked at him. "I don't know if that will work or not. I just know that since I've been released I feel like I'm going to explode with everything around me moving too fast. People too close to me. I'm trying my best to deal with it, but I'm overwhelmed. I want to go back, some days, and be put in a cell where I can't hear or feel."

He moved toward her, and when she didn't back away, he pulled her into his arms and held her. When she grabbed onto his arms and held him, he could feel her sorrow and her pain. Touching her arms, the bare skin exposed from her shirt, he felt the power of her like he'd picked up a live wire while standing in a puddle of water. But he didn't let her go.

When she dug her nails into his arms, he knew that he was going to pass out. It wasn't painful, but it was a lot of information. He could see Mr. Rogers sitting in his chair, crying about how lonely he was. Mrs. Betts yelling at the children next door for making too much noise. All she wanted was for them to come and visit her when her own grandchildren wouldn't. There was Mrs. Windle down the street, who took a walk every day to see what sort of mischief she could get into to have the police come and visit her. There were more people needing friendship, someone to talk to and to be with. And because they were so alone, they didn't want to live. Felt useless.

"They're all lonely. And they're scared." Carter told him that she knew, but for him to look deeper. That was when he saw things that he could never un-see. Women being abused by not just spouses, but their children as well. Humans that were cruel to each other in ways that sickened him. Animals, pets really, starving from being left outside and no one feeding them. He was bombarded with people's pain, with their thoughts and actions. Then it was all gone when Carter let him go.

It was painful to think that all this was going on right in his own town. That these people were suffering for reasons that could easily be taken care of or fixed. He reached for Carter again, thinking to hold her, when she took another step back. It occurred to him what she was doing and trying to keep him from seeing too.

"You only gave me a taste of what you feel." She nodded, and he watched her face. "What if I told you that we can help these people? Some of them, anyway. They only need companionship, and perhaps a friend."

"And the others? How do we help them? How do we help them so that I can have peace?" Josh told her that he didn't know. "If I touch you, you're going to feel what I feel. Don't you understand that? We can't be mates, it'll tear you apart. Just as it does me. I thought that sleeping with you might be a way to get this to work. But I can see now that it would have been a major mistake. I might hurt you with too much information that I know about people."

He pulled her to him then, holding her tightly until she didn't struggle anymore. And when she went limp in his arms, he looked down into her face and smiled. She said she was sorry.

"For what? Showing me in the only way you know how what is going on? I thank you for that. I could never have understood without that. Holding you, being your rock, is what I'd really like to do." Carter told him that it was too much. "Perhaps for me, and I can't imagine what it is for you, but I want to help you. I want us to help the others as much as we can."

"How?" He pulled her along with him to the desk, and sat her on his lap while he called his brother, Evan. He did it this way so that she could hear the conversation as well. "I have some information for you, and I'd like to help you with it." Evan asked what sort of information. He told him what he'd felt and knew about some of the people in town. "Can we get them help? Some of them, it seems like they just need a friend. I was thinking that we could have the younger pups and others in Nate's pack be companions to some of the elderly that are lonely."

"I've talked to Mr. Rogers a couple of times when he shows up at the clinic. He really is in a bad way most of the time. Not so much his age and it pulling him down, but like you said, he's very lonely. I think that's an excellent idea. What else did you have in mind?"

They talked for another two hours. Carter gave them names and information that he'd not gotten. Most of the people were the elderly, some of them were even leap members. This fix he could help her with. The rest of it, he'd have to figure out just what she needed and get it for her. After hanging up from talking to Evan, she didn't move off his lap but laid back on his chest with her head on his shoulder.

"When we were little, Rachel and I used to talk about a knight in shining armor coming to save us. He'd be on this white horse and he'd slay the bad people that were around us, and we'd be free to live in the castle with him for the rest of our lives." He kissed her on the shoulder and asked her what she thought of now. "The same things, only my knight has a face now. And my castle is this home. But I'm afraid of getting you hurt."

"I know that, honey. Most of the time, what you can do, it frightens me as well. Not that I believe you'll hurt me in any way, but you're so very powerful, I worry about what will happen to you if someone comes for you." She told him that they were, her parents. "Yes, well, they're never going to get close enough to you to take or harm you. And they'll regret the day that they fucked with this family."

"They don't know what I can do. Not all of it." He didn't figure that they did. Otherwise they might have backed off. Josh told her that. "No, they would have come regardless. Their thinking is that there isn't any way that I'd be able to hurt them. That they have some sort of free pass to me because they're my parents. Not that they like being my parents — they're just thinking that it will save them if it comes to that."

"Carter, have you ever hurt someone and didn't mean it? Other than the guard, who very much deserved what he got. I mean, you couldn't have known how to use this power much when you were younger." She nodded but didn't speak. "Was it Rachel?"

"Yes. She was in pain from being beaten by my dad. He'd told her, I suppose several times, that they had no money for a trip that she wanted to go on at school. I knew that he had enough for her to go, and money for her to buy a nice trinket too. So I decided to go and get it for her, so that she could go. But on the way to his room, Mom caught me by the arm and I freaked out at what I saw in her mind. Rachel heard us screaming—it was hurting Mom too, I guess—and Rachel touched me. It threw her across the room, and she hit her head badly enough to need stitches." He asked her how that was explained to the doctor. "I don't think even my mom knew what had happened at that point. She thought that with all the anger that we had, it might have made Rachel slip and fall. That wasn't it—I did it. I hurt her."

Josh just held her, enjoying that they were trying to work this out, but no less scared for her when her parents came. The longer they sat there, not speaking but just being together, he realized that she was falling asleep.

Adjusting her in his arms, he held her while he went to the couch, laying her down on it. He took off her shoes and his own and joined her. It was tight on the sofa, and he decided that they needed a deeper one, but once he was behind her, spooned in with her on the couch, he closed his eyes, thinking that he'd only lay there for a moment or two. But she was warm and comfortable, so he felt himself drifting off in sleep as well.

At some point he felt her moving. Pulling her closer to him, he buried his chin into her neck. The scent of her was calming to his cat, and he started to drift off again when he felt her terror. Not knowing what it was, he tried to comfort her again when he saw what she was seeing.

The child couldn't have been more than a few months old. The blanket over her was a bright pink yet stained with dirt and something else. When the image pulled back, sort of like a movie would when you could see more of the scene, he saw that the baby was laying by the side of the road by a mailbox. It took him several seconds to realize what he was seeing. An abandoned baby. Suddenly a car came out of nowhere and was heading right for the child and mailbox. The screams woke him before he saw what happened to the child.

"We have to go." He nodded, still trying to wrap his head around the car and what it would have done to the child. Carter was pulling on her shoes when she told him again that they had to go. "She needs us to get her."

He hurried then, but he didn't know where they were going. Or if the child was really there. As soon as he was in the car, he turned to her. Fear was there, and he could almost feel it.

"Where are we going?" Carter told him the address even as he was pulling out of the driveway. "Was that real? Is there a child in a ditch?"

"Yes. They didn't want her anymore, and if we can get to her before they come back to kill her, we'll be able to save her." He drove a little faster, knowing that he'd get pulled over if he wasn't careful. "How did you know? I've never.... How did you know that she was there?"

"I saw it with you. By holding you, I was able to see it too. But I didn't see an address. I missed that."

They were almost to the mailbox, and he could see the car that had been going toward the child in the vision pulling away after dropping off the baby. As soon as he was level with the box, Carter jumped out, snatched up the baby with the bright pink blanket, and got back in the car.

Josh pulled into the drive across from the mail box and they looked her over. He could smell the drugs on her, and knew that they'd given her something so that she'd not feel anything. When the car came back, speeding like he'd seen it, they hit the ditch then the mailbox before they flipped upside down several times, coming to a stop a hundred yards or so from where the child had been.

~~~

Dylan didn't know what was going on, why both Josh and Carter were not saying much, but she had two dead people in the car and an infant that more than likely didn't belong to them. She went to talk to Carter, figuring she would have the most information.

"Did you know who they were?" She shook her head, and kept looking at the ambulance where the baby was being checked out by Evan. "Did you see this?"

Carter looked at her, fearful again, but she nodded. "We both did. Josh was sleeping with me when I saw it. We came here to save the baby, but I didn't know the couple." Dylan asked her if it was their child, knowing that it wasn't. "I didn't see that part. I'm sorry. I do know that they drugged her and that they didn't want her anymore. They were thinking that if they killed her, no one would know that they'd done this."

"Well, that worked out so well for them." Carter smiled; it was the first time Dylan had seen her do that since she'd met her. "They were both high on something—we've yet to determine what. The child is going to have to go to the hospital, I would imagine, then child services will need to find her parents. Can you tell me who they are by chance?"

"I might be able to. May I hold her to see?" Dylan walked to the ambulance with her, Josh right behind her. Dylan was glad to see Josh so supportive of Carter, even if he did look as confused as she felt. When Carter was handed the baby from Evan, he told her that she was going to be fine. They'd given her some kind of sedative, but not enough to do much more than put her to sleep for a little while longer.

61

Carter held the child, then unwrapped her blanket. When she hesitated for a moment, Dylan watched her until she looked at her.

"What happens to her if she has no one?" Dylan asked her if she could see that. "I haven't touched her yet. I don't.... What will happen to her if there isn't anyone that wants her? Will she go into the system?"

"More than likely. After she spends a few days in the hospital to make sure that she has no ill effects from whatever they gave her. They'll also see if she'd been abused prior to that." Carter nodded, but still didn't touch her. "Are you afraid of what you might find?"

"Yes."

It was enough of an answer that Dylan's heart broke for her. She wanted to take the child from her and tell her that she'd find another way. Also, she wanted to hold the other woman and tell her that she'd fix whatever she could to make her happy again.

Carter touched the baby's cheek, then put her tiny hand into hers. As soon as the baby wrapped her fingers around her larger one, the little girl opened her eyes and looked right at her. Dylan was both glad and afraid of what she might have gone through in her short life.

"This isn't the first time that she's been drugged. When she cries, they give her Benadryl so that she'll shut up. It makes her sick, and they hurt her when she is." Evan asked how she had ended up with the other couple. "I can see her mother's face, and that of her father. They make her smile, and she is glad when they come to her. Beth, her name is Beth, and she was kidnapped a week ago when her mother was walking down the street with her in the stroller. The man held a gun to her head while the woman took the child."

"Do you have a name for the parents?" Dylan couldn't believe that she'd gotten this much information, and even how it had happened. When Carter frowned, she thought that she'd gotten all that she could. Then Josh stepped up behind Carter and touched the child as well.

"Elizabeth and Samuel Farrell. They're from Columbus. The kidnapping happened not two blocks from where they live." Josh gave them the address and Dylan wrote it down. "They're frantic with worry, and the police told them that after the first twenty-four hours, then the chances get slimmer and slimmer in finding her alive. Someone should shoot them for saying that to them."

"I agree." She pulled out her cell and made a call. In seconds she had not just their address, but also some of the news about their child. She asked Evan if she could tell them their child was safe and here. "I don't want them to get here and find out that she's been abused any more than what you've already told me."

"She's malnourished and has some bruising. But if you're asking me if she was sexually abused, I can tell you that she hasn't been. Not her mouth nor any other part of her body." Dylan didn't want to think about what he meant by her mouth. There were a lot of sick fucks out in the world. "Yes, I'd make the call and tell them that you found her. Then you'd better come up with a good reason for knowing that it was their child. Because you can't say that you had Carter tell you."

"Agent Hutch? You might want to come and look at this." She walked to the car the bodies had been taken from. They had been on drugs for some time if their needle marks were any indication. "We were going through the glove box when we found this. It's a list. And I'm pretty sure that they have done this before. And from the looks of it, were going to continue to do it as well."

The names were listed by dates. Each name above the Farrell's was marked with an 'X' with the date. For the past four months, they had snatched a child from someone every two weeks or so. Looking at Carter when she came to where she was standing, she gave her the list when she put out her hand. When she handed it back to her after a few minutes, she said that they were all dead. All the children were dead that were on the list above the Farrell child. Ten babies had lost their lives because of those two people.

Dylan made the call. It was a good one—she was happy to be able to tell the couple that they'd found their child, and their joy at being able to come and see her. Dylan explained that she'd have to spend a couple of days in the hospital due to being slightly drugged, but they could see her while they were there. After she made arrangements to speak to them in person, Dylan closed her phone and looked at Carter.

"Thank you, Carter. I couldn't have done this without you. And if you hadn't done what you did with Josh, then she would surely have died as well. Maybe even more children." Carter nodded and looked at the ambulance again where the baby was. "Do you want to go to the hospital with her?"

"I can't go there. Hospitals are too much for me." Dylan nodded, completely understanding. "I won't always have time to tell you before I go to help someone. Like today, it was go or she'd be dead. But I'll let you know if I can. Is that all right?"

"Yes, always. And if you have to do what you did today, you do it. Don't wait for the police, or someone to tell you that

64

it's all right to touch someone. You save who you can when you can." Carter nodded and thanked her. "How much does it cost you when something like this comes to you? A great deal?"

"Today, with Josh holding me, it was easier to sort through what was happening and where it was. The information coming at me wasn't muddled in my mind because I was so afraid. He calmed me, in ways that no one else has ever done before." Dylan told her that was what a mate could do for her. "I didn't know that. I thought...I guess I thought it would only benefit them in some way."

"You mean sexually." Her face turned pink when she nodded. "Yes, that is something that they enjoy, and let me tell you, they're fantastic at it too. I think once you and Josh have gotten straightened out what you need from him and start to come to terms with what you can do, I think everything will go so much better for you both."

They both watched as the ambulance took off for the hospital. The family would take at least another hour to get there, and Evan had gone with Beth to make sure that she got the best of care. Not that she wouldn't anyway, but he was very thorough about his patients.

"Where are you going, in case I need something answered?" Carter said that she'd be at Josh's house. That she was going to stay there from now on. "Good. Why don't the two of you come over for dinner tomorrow night? I love seeing you guys, and I know that Josh has a little more free time on his hands right now."

"Yes, when Carol called him today about a listing, I thought he'd go to work. But he told her that he wasn't working and almost hung up on her. I think he needs this

65

very much." Dylan thought they both did, but said nothing. "I can read your mind, you know."

"I know. And I understand that it's a habit that you have, and it's more than likely saved your ass more than a few times. But if you want to know something, ask me. All right?" Carter told her she was sorry. "There isn't any reason for you to be sorry, Carter. You didn't think about it. You're not malicious when you do it, and I don't even feel it. But I'd rather you didn't."

"I won't. But please, don't lie to me or keep things from me that you think might upset me. I might not like whatever it is you want me to do, but don't lie to me about it. I'm trying my best to fit into a world that I've been away from for over a decade. I need help, I'm aware of that. Everyday something new comes to me. Cell phones, computers that are small enough to fit in your hand. I've missed so much. It's hard for me to acclimate myself to it all." Dylan hadn't thought of that, how much she was going to have to learn. She told her she was sorry. "I am as well. Thank you for coming so quickly today. I'm not sure that we could have handled all this had you not."

"It was my pleasure. And as I said before, your mate can help you a great deal in all that you need. And if he helped you today, then that's all the more reason for you to trust him to help you again and again." Carter nodded at her, but was still not convinced, she could tell. "I'm headed back. I'll see you tomorrow night for dinner then."

Dylan had a feeling that things were going to change for the couple. She was glad. Carter needed someone to love her, and she couldn't think of anyone better at the job for her than Josh. He was the kindest man she knew, and the most gentle.

They'd be fine after today. She was also having someone look into the prison for her. Those people were going to be in the cells next to those that they hurt before the end of the week, or she'd go there and take care of them herself. And they'd be sorry if she had to do that.

Joshua

Chapter 5

Josh didn't want to go up to bed. It was lonely there, and he wanted to hold Carter so that she'd not have bad thoughts or dreams. He had thought of nothing else but holding her earlier today, and he wanted to do it again. Well, more than hold her, he wanted to make her his and make love to her.

Going up the stairs, he realized that he was pouting and laughed. What a dumbass, he thought to himself. A grown man pouting because he had to sleep by himself. It wasn't as if he'd not been doing that for a while now, but he wanted—

"Hello." Carter was standing at the top of the stairs when he made it to the landing. He told her hello back. "I was wondering something. If we have sex and I'm terrible at it, will you still sleep with me?"

"You mean will I go to my lonely bed with my lonely covers and lonely pillows?" She laughed, and he smiled. Her laugh was rusty, because he knew that she'd not had an occasion to laugh much. "Yes. I'd want to sleep with you after making love with you. That way I could make love to you

69

throughout the night whenever we woke up. And you cannot make me believe that you'd be anything but fantastic at it."

"No, I'm not too terribly good at it. I only had it the one time before they locked me away, and it wasn't all that enjoyable." He asked her how old she'd been. "Seventeen. I had sex for the first time the night I was arrested. We sort of didn't have a lot of room. And I think he was in somewhat of a hurry. When it was over I thought that sex was highly overrated and decided that it wasn't worth the work someone had to put into it."

"What sort of work did you have to do?" She giggled, and he smiled. "Hearing you laugh and giggle makes my heart sing. I'm going to try and make you do it more often. Anyway, what was the work?"

"Getting undressed, for one. I had more clothing on than he did, and he wasn't very practiced. Not any more than I was, I guess. He tried to take my bra off like he did my shirt. Up and over my head." Josh could just see it, two teenagers fumbling around trying to have sex. "Of course, then it got all tangled up in my hair and I had to have him stop for a moment. While I had my head buried in my shirt, he was tweaking my breasts. I wanted to smack him. It doesn't sound like I enjoyed it at all, does it?"

"Not really. When you want to smack your partner before he even does the deed, then that's a bad omen." He moved closer, but didn't rush her like he wanted. "Did you climax? I mean, was there any kind of peak in this for you?"

"Not really. It was okay. About the time I was getting some kind of good feeling from it, he came. It wasn't his fault, at least that's what he told me. It was mine because I rushed him along. If anything, I wanted him to slow it down. Are you going to kiss me, Josh?" He shook his head and stood in front of her, standing toe to toe. "Oh. I thought that you'd want to."

"You kiss me. If I kiss you then I'm going to devour you. You set the pace by kissing me the way you want." She only stared at him. "I want you badly, Carter. I could toss you to the floor right now and have my way with you."

"Will you fumble?" He shook his head and smiled at her. "No, you'd not fumble at all, would you? You'd be perfection at sex even with boring old me. And unselfish too, wouldn't you? I think having sex with you would never be boring, nor would it be a quickie, would it?"

"No, never with you. But for you, I'd be all those things and more." He needed to kiss her, and lowered his head until he could feel her breath on his lips. See her lashes as they fanned out over her eyes. Her eyes were the most incredible shade of light brown, with tiny specks of blue in them. There was nothing about this woman that was ordinary or boring. "You are perfection to me. The way you're shy around my family. The way you tilt your head when you're trying to figure something out. There's the way that you curl and uncurl your toes in the carpet when you're in your bare feet. I love how you sit all prim and proper with your hands in your lap and watch people."

"That last one is to not touch anyone." Josh grinned and brushed his mouth softly over hers. "I'm wet and needy. Please, kiss me, then take me to bed."

Instead of kissing her, he picked her up in his arms and carried her to the bedroom. Dropping her on the new mattress, he laughed when she did. Toeing off his shoes, he watched her for any sign that she wasn't really ready. Josh was—he thought that he could break concrete, he was so hard. But he'd never hurt her or touch her in any way that would frighten or hurt her. He knew better than most what she'd been through, and he was going to make sure that she enjoyed being with him as much as he did with her.

When she sat up on the side of the bed, she helped him pull his clothing off. His shirt was first, then his belt. As he unsnapped his pants, she reached into them and wrapped her hand around him. His moan came from his feet as she fisted him. This was going to go much quicker than he thought if only her hand touching him could make him this close.

The kiss that she gave him was timid and soft, unlike the way she was treating his cock. Her hand was tight around him, painfully so. When he undid the rest of his snaps, Josh pulled his pants down to his thighs. Carter moaned against his chest, where she was nibbling on his nipple. He could almost taste her need now, and wanted to help her in any way that she'd allow him to.

"I'm going to come standing here just like this if you keep that up." Carter feasted on his other nipple, not stopping at all in fisting his cock. "Baby, I'm so close to the edge right now. Wouldn't you rather I was inside of you when I come?"

"Yes."

He shredded her nightgown and asked her to lay back. Her body was more than he'd thought it was—everything about her was soft yet firm. Cupping her breasts in his hands, he leaned over her and suckled at them, darting back and forth as he sampled them both. His cock was right at her entrance, her heat pulling at him. And when he slid just his crown into her, she bowed up off the bed and screamed out her release.

"Christ, that was amazing." She told him she was sorry. "Don't ever be sorry for taking your pleasure, baby. Watching you come like that, you have no idea what that does to me. Do it again for me. Come while I watch you."

He hadn't entered her yet, just the tip of his cock seemed to be enough for her for now. Josh watched her come four more times. Each time her screams were loud enough to wake the household, but he didn't care. And when she begged him for more, Josh moved forward, taking his time so that he'd not hurt her.

Fucking her this way was killing him. But each time she cried out her joy, he knew that he could do this all night for her. And when she pulled his mouth to her, he kissed her hungrily and told her how much he loved her, how happy he was that she was his.

"You want to mark me? Bite me?"

He nudged her throat, then licked the pounding pulse there with his tongue. It felt like it was running at top speed — he was barely able to tell one beat from the next, and when he nipped none too gently at her flesh, he wrapped her legs around his hips and took her hard.

His own climax was pounding at him relentlessly. Sweat beaded at his back and his chest. When she screamed out her release, he bit down on her throat and tasted her hot spicy blood, and came hard himself while she screamed over and over with one release right after the other.

It wasn't enough for him; he needed her to mark him as well. Giving her his throat, begging her to bite him too, he felt her teeth graze over his skin and nearly cried out with the pleasure of it. And then when she bit him, Josh blinked out for a moment, his mind simply shutting down when he came for the third time.

Josh didn't remember getting into the bed. He was lying

atop Carter, who was unconscious or asleep—either way she was down for the count as much as he was. Moving around to adjust them so that they could be in the middle and turned the right way, he had to lie down twice to catch his breath, it had taken so much out of him. Christ, she might just kill him after one night of making love to her.

Finally they were both with their heads at the top of the bed. He didn't know what had happened to the pillows, so he laid her head on his arm. He knew that she was all right; her breathing was steady now, and her heart rate had slowed. So, when he curled around her body, he closed his eyes and let sleep take him under.

This time he knew that she was having the dream, and paid attention to what was going on. There was a man and a woman, and they were arguing about the money. It occurred to him then that these were her parents, and that this was in real time.

"She's going to make us so much money, and in the end, it'll just be me and you, like it should have been all along." Her father—Lee, Josh thought his name was—nodded while Hazel Compton went on about selling off Carter. "That man who gave us the first part of his payment for her, do you think he'll get pissy when we take her to the third man? Not that it matters—we're going to kill him when we see him anyway. Or have Carter do it. She'll do it too—we'll tell her that he's doing something to us, and she'll want to save us. You think that too?"

"They've always hated me, and more so because they could never get to Rachel. They wanted to sell her off too, but for entirely different reasons. They were going to be her pimps, and they thought that she'd be good at sleeping around. For the same reason they hope that I'll save them, they thought that Rachel would agree." He looked at Carter when she appeared in the room with him. "I've never been able to do this before. Be in the same room with someone I was listening to. Dylan said that I could use you to help me. She was right. You're making me stronger in this."

"I'm assuming that they haven't any idea we're here." Carter shook her head and started looking around the room. Josh could see that she was actually moving things, and he tried the same thing. "What are we looking for? I'm assuming it has something to do with this hotel."

"Where they are. I can't pinpoint them when I'm watching them from a distance. It would help us if I knew how much more time I had." He nodded and looked around. Then he realized they were in a cheap hotel room, and moved through the door to the outside to see the name of the place. Coming back in, he told her where they were and how far they were from them. "So, we have about two days to get ready."

"I can maybe slow them down a bit more if I can do things to their car. I mean, in this shape, I'm not sure what it would be, but I'm betting that I could do something." She grinned at him and he fell in love with Carter again. "Do you have a knife?"

"Just think of one."

He did and felt one fill his hand. Going outdoors again, he opened the switch blade and rammed the blade into the tires. Having one flat might not stop them for very long, so he cut all four of them.

Sticking his head into the trunk to slice the spare tire, he saw the ropes and chains there. Also, the guns. They were coming, and weren't going to take any chances in not being able to take Carter with them when they did. Going back to the room, he watched as Carter looked at her parents.

"I've not seen them in ten years. You'd think that I'd feel something for them. I mean, besides contempt." He stood next to her and took her hand into his. "This is all very strange, being here. Do you suppose it'll be like this all the time when we're together?"

"I don't know. I guess we'll have to figure this out on our own." He told her what he'd found in the trunk. "I cut up the rope, which was surprisingly easy. And the guns I took and threw into the dumpster across the lot. The chains as well. That's another thing to think about. How we can move through the walls and doors, but I can touch things like what was in the trunk to dispose of."

"We'll figure it out. And if we don't, then that's all right as well. I'm not as afraid either. I feel calm right now. And it's because of you, I'm thinking. I've never felt that way before either." He told her that he loved her. "I think I might love you as well. But I'm not sure. I've never been loved before by anyone—I love Rachel, but I don't think that is the same thing as loving you."

"No, not at all. But I can live with that for now."

He kissed her on the hand and could feel himself being pulled away. For some reason he thought that he'd be right back in their bed, but he wasn't. He was standing in a room no bigger than a medium sized closet. There wasn't a door, but bars across the front of it and over the window. And sitting on the bed was Carter.

He noticed that she wasn't with him this time, and he worried a little. But when she turned and looked where he was standing, he had a moment of panic. It was then that he saw that someone had shoved a tray into her cell, and she got up to get it. The woman at the bars spoke before he could wonder why she wasn't eating with the other inmates.

"Ten more days, Compton, then you can go back into the population. Next time you have trouble with another inmate, you tell me. I'll plunk her ass. All right?"

Carter told her thanks and she moved on. He wondered how many times she'd been confined to her room when something happened. As he was being pulled again he looked around at the starkness of the room and his heart hurt.

This time he was in the bed, Carter curled up next to him. The sun was just making itself known through the curtains, and he wondered at the time. Lying back down, he held Carter tighter and closed his eyes. He was going to have a lot of questions when they finally got up. It might not be early in the morning like when he usually woke, but they were together, and that's all that mattered.

~~~

Carter sat on the chair that was on the deck and looked out over the back yard. It was beautiful, something that she'd never dreamed of having. The pool was covered now, but she would bet in the summer months it would be warm and sunny back here. There wasn't any furniture back here either, just the one chair that the new butler had brought out for her when he saw her standing here.

The door behind her opened and closed, and she could smell the fresh coffee. George had asked her if she liked it strong or weak, and she'd told him where she'd been for the last ten years. Nodding at her, he told her tar. Laughing with him, his wife, Ada, asked her if she could make her up something to eat. She told her whatever they were having was all right with her.

Picking up the mug from the tray that had fresh fruit and warm muffins on it, she thanked him for both the chair and the food. He nodded once at her, and told her that the elder Mr. Whitfield was going to join her soon. He was in the kitchen.

She thought it would be Oliver, but it was Ollie, his father. When he brought out his own chair, she told him that Josh had to run into town for a little while, something about the sale of a house that he'd been working on.

"They only wanted him. And he told me that he'd not do it for anyone else but this couple. They're expecting their first child too." Ollie nodded and took one of the muffins as they sat staring out at the trees. "Are you here for a reason? Or just wanted to come for a visit?"

"Both. I have me a reason, but I did want to come and see you. Josh told me that you were up and about, and I thought I'd come see you and ask you a question." Carter told him she was glad for the company and to ask away. "You don't have to answer me if you don't want to. I have lots of questions that people don't answer for me. I wonder if they think I'm too addled to remember the answers or not understand what they're talking about. That's usually what it is, but I don't tell them that." She cleared her throat and he smiled. "I do go on, don't I?"

"I really was clearing my throat. It's a little rough this morning." She didn't tell him from all the screams that Josh had made her do, or that she'd been hoarse when she'd first got up. Carter asked him what he needed.

"Okay. I find myself going to pawn shops all the time. Ain't usually anything there that I want or need, but I took a look at the jewelry this time. I've been skipping that since my wife passed." She told him she was sorry. "Me too. I loved her like she was my air when I was breathing in and out, and there wasn't nothing that could have replaced it. But I found this piece of jewelry, and I was wondering if you could tell me something about it. If you don't want to that's fine too, but I was curious about it is all."

He handed her the bracelet and she held it in her hands. All sorts of memories came with it; the warmest ones were from the man sitting next to her. Ollie had wanted to give it to his beloved, then remembered that she was gone and almost didn't buy it. But in the end, he bought it because he was going to give it to Eve.

"The last woman that wore it was elderly. It was given to her by her husband, who passed when he was a very young man. He left her alone in a world full of men who thought that she was too stupid to run an empire." Ollie asked her what empire. "I don't know yet. I have to find his string."

"I'm assuming that means you have to find people by the way they're on something." Carter told him that was right. That she'd never told anyone that before, and was glad that he understood. "You go on there and find out who her beloved is."

She could feel the children who touched it, the way they loved how it sparkled in the sunlight. Carter told Ollie everything that she felt and what the faces of the children looked like as well.

"He loved her so very much. The bracelet was made from a necklace that his mother had. The woman's name is Bea, and she didn't care to wear things around her neck. They would tangle in her hair. So, he commissioned for it to be made into three bracelets of different colored stones so that she could wear them all together or separately."

"I wonder where the other two are." She knew. When she passed over one of the diamonds, she could feel Bea's pain and sorrow again. "Maybe I'll try and find them."

"You won't, I'm sorry to say. Bea put one of them in the coat pocket of her true love when he was laid out in the living room when he died. He'd had a heart attack at the age of thirty-four. The rubies, for all the love that her heart spilled when he left her." She heard his sniffle at that, so she continued with the third one. "They had but one child—her name was Emerald, like the sea. Her eyes were the same color as her father's, the green of the sea she'd been named for. She died when she was six—her little body was found near the ocean that she so loved to play in. Emerald had drowned."

"You wove me a good tale there, but it's about as sad as I've ever heard. I was going to give it to Eve to make my son a little jealous, but I'm not going to now." She asked him why not. "Because of the deaths around it."

"You should give it to her anyway. So that the next time the bracelet is touched by someone like me, they can see that among all the sorrow, a wonderful woman wore it and it made her happy." Ollie just stared at her, and she told him she was sorry. "I just read what was on it. I didn't think that it would be too sad for you."

"You did me a right favor by doing it. I can't thank you enough. And I think you're right about giving it to Eve. And I'll tell her the story about it too. She'll think that it's romantic or something like that." Carter told him that she thought it was as well. "There you go. She'll love the story that goes with it, and how you and I thought that she should wear it to make happy memories."

"You don't have to tell her I was involved." Ollie told her she'd know. "Why would she know if you don't tell her? Don't, let it come from you."

"She'll know that I'm not the romantic type, and that someone told me the tale anyways." He stood up. "Thank you very much, Carter. You've made this old man very happy by doing this for me."

Carter hadn't wanted to do the bracelet when he'd first pulled it out. She was afraid that it would have something on it where she would have nightmares about. Sitting there, thinking about what her and Josh had done last night by going to see her parents, she had to wonder if it was him or was she just using more of her brain to work things out. Knowing the little bit about what she could do had made her afraid to try different things. Now she wanted to play.

Drinking the last of her coffee, she went into the yard where if she were to mess up, there wouldn't be anything around that she'd hurt or break. Since she'd never been showy about what she could do, she just stood there quietly and reached out beyond where she was standing for any sign of life. The first thing she touched was the pack master, Nate.

Do I know you? She told him who she was and who she was mated to. *Do you mind telling me how you're doing this?*

I have this bit of power, and I was stretching my mind to see what else I could do. He told her that was a good idea. *I didn't mean to bother you.*

It's fine. We've lost a pup and I'm trying to locate him. He's three and wandered off from the playground where he was playing. She asked Nate what his name was. *Lesley Luna. His father is Lesley as well. Can you find him?*

I can try. Just tell me how long he's been missing. Nate told her

81

only about twenty minutes. *Okay, so he wouldn't have traveled far. Let me look.*

It took her five frustrating minutes to find him. He was at the back of the property, and he'd been hurt when he fell down a hill. She guided Nate to him by landmarks that she could see since she didn't know the area, that's all she could do. And when Nate found the little boy, he was as thankful as Ollie had been about the bracelet.

I owe you, Carter. You've probably saved his life. There are poachers around, and if they would have come upon him, there is no telling what they might have done to him. She told him there were three strangers on his land now. Guiding him to them, she told him that they were looking for prey, humans to hunt. *The same thing that Josh told me about when he was finishing up his house. Thank you. You've told me where they're coming in from as well. Tell Josh I'll talk to him later.*

Carter kept a tab on the three men. One of them didn't want to be there—he thought this was all wrong and was going to demand his money back. The second man was excited. He'd never killed a person before, and thought it would be a hoot to run one down and shoot it in the head. It was well worth the five grand that he'd paid the man, Moody, to have the chance. The last man was Moody, and he was nervous. Stretching her wings, so to speak, she decided to speak to the second man and send him images of dead men that had been shot.

Not knowing if it would do any good, she bombarded the man with image after image. She knew that he was in pain but didn't stop or slow down. When he moved away from her touch, she had a moment of her own fear, thinking that she might have killed him. But he saw the wolf pack then and turned and ran. She didn't think he'd be back, despite wanting to run down a human to kill them before she entered his head. It was no longer as appealing as it had been to him.

Going into the house when she couldn't feel anyone else around, she stopped by the kitchen again to drop off her plate and mug. She warned them both about people with guns on the property before going into the office to play on the computer. This was the most exciting thing that she'd missed, she thought.

Chapter 6

Hazel wondered what the hell had happened. All their tires were slashed up like they'd been targeted by a bunch of hooligans. She asked Lee for the fourth time what they were supposed to do now.

"I don't know, Hazel. Christ, how many times are you going to ask me that and have me give you the same damned answer? I don't fucking know. Even though we have the money to buy the tires, there is the added problem that we don't have any way of getting the car there to have it done. And the tow truck wants two hundred dollars to put it up on one of them tow things and take it someplace." She didn't even ask him if he was going to pay it. He'd better. "He said it would take him an hour to get here. Until then, we have to wait. You didn't call the police, did you?"

"Do I look stupid to you? Also, where the hell are all our things? The ropes are gone, so are all the chains. And how the hell did they get the guns out of there without being seen by someone? We're going to need those too. How did they get in the trunk without a damned key?" When he didn't answer her, she felt her temper get a little hotter. But he defused it in a second when he reached down and plucked a dandelion out of the cracks of the place and handed to her. "Thank you. I think both our tempers could use a break."

"I was thinking the same thing. How about we walk over that to that restaurant and have us a nice breakfast, and then come back here? The wait won't feel so long if we got something else to think about." She told him that was a great idea. "Yeah, I come up with them on occasion. Not too often though. I don't want you to think I'm some sort of genius or something."

They had an hour and they were going to make the best of it. But instead of eating there where they could be waited on, they got it to go and took it to the room. It was more enjoyable that way; the food fight that they had in the room was much funnier knowing that someone else would have to clean it up. And right on time, the towing service showed up.

"Somebody doesn't like you much." Hazel heard Lee asked him why. "Well, I've seen one or two tires slashed up, but all four of them? They had to have some powerful hate on you. Not to mention, you have any idea how much effort it takes to stab a tire and then slice it? That's gotta be tiring for someone to do that."

They had just thought it was kids having a night out. But she noticed that they were the only ones with tires that had been cut. And all four. Now she had to think who might know that they were staying there, and who would hate them enough to do such a thing. They'd not bothered anyone that she could remember. And they stayed by themselves when they had to go out.

Everybody liked them. They were the life of any party they went to. And if you got a few too many beers in Lee, he could be made to do just about anything that would bring out a laugh or two from everyone. The first person that came to mind that might hate them that much was Carter. But that wasn't possible. She didn't know they were coming after her.

They had to ride over to the shop that was putting new tires on with the tow guy. It was crowded in the cab with him, him being a fat slob of a person, but she didn't want to take a cab and then have to pay for it. It was going to be hard enough to get their things out of the hotel room without paying for damages as it was. However, it kept coming back to Carter hating them enough to slash their tires.

When things were set up with the shop that was putting four new tires on the car, she sat with Lee in the little waiting room and asked him what he thought about it. The first thing he said was, it was kids. But then she pointed out that theirs was the only car.

"You think Carter knows." He shook his head. "It's been a long time since we seen her. She might have gotten some more of those freaky things that she can do. And I don't believe for a minute that it's all her mind. She never was all that smart. I mean, look how easy we got her to take the fall for us."

"I know, but she'd have to be powerful, don't you think? Just to come here and slash up the tires. No, you're worrying over nothing. It had to be kids." But she could tell that he was mulling it over now. "She might have told someone to come here and do it. Instead of coming here herself, don't you think? I mean, that still doesn't figure in how she knew we'd be here nor what kind of car we drove. It just doesn't add up. No, it was just a bunch of random kids that took turns slashing the tires for us."

"But she's been someplace she could practice that shit she could do. What if, during that time, she was able to develop something else? For all we know she can fly now." That would mean more money for them, if that was the case. "I'm telling you right now, Lee, we're going to make a killing off them girls. I just hope that we don't have to kill Rachel right off. If Carter is stronger, we're going to have to do some big time explaining to calm her, so she doesn't use her shit for hurting us. She won't kill us, I know that—we're her parents. But she could hurt us up a little. I don't like to mention this, but maybe we should pick up something to knock her out. I don't want her doped up when those people come to have a look at what she can do, do you?"

"We'll just tell her that she'll go back to prison if she hurts us. Like you said, we're her parents. I know we weren't around much, and she has to know that we set her up in that robbery. But we killed that cop, and that isn't going to get us any goodwill with anyone should she say something to them. I'm really surprised that she's not said anything up to now. She sure had enough time to do something about it, don't you think?" Hazel asked what Carter could say. "I don't know, honey, but I'd sure hate to end up behind bars when we have all these plans about making some fast money. What do you suppose they want her for? Those people that we're selling her to."

"A weapon, I guess. All we had to tell them was a few white lies and they believed us. I don't think they would have cared one tiny bit if all we told them that she could do was move a book around and bend up a spoon. You coming up with the fact that she could lift up cars was about the best,

I think." Hazel laughed as she continued. "Of course, like I said, all we ever knew she could do was lift a few books off the shelf, and after we beat her a little, she told us she could bend some spoons. Not really a big deal, but that was enough to get their attention."

Again, Hazel wondered if she'd gotten any stronger. That worried her enough that she was thinking of ways to get Lee to go to her instead of both of them. If he got hurt, then she'd still be able to go after the money when she got Carter to go with one of the buyers for her. And if she did hurt her dad, then maybe she'd feel badly enough that she'd cooperate with her. Laughing, she thought of Carter doing anything that they wanted her to. She was ten kinds of stubborn.

When the car was ready, they left and headed to the hotel. Their things were packed up, so all she had to do was run in, get their suitcases and stuff, and they'd be on their way. But the maid had already been in the room while they were gone, and she'd taken their luggage after cleaning up the room. They were so fucked right now.

"Why would she do that?" Lee sat with her in the car after she told him what had happened. "I mean, was there a note or anything?"

"Oh shit." She pulled the envelope out of her pocket and handed it to him. "I thought it was a bill or something, because the room had been cleaned up of our mess. You think it's telling us where our stuff is? Because that would be nice to get going."

He opened it up and then handed it to her. It said that they'd taken their things to the office and to get them, they'd have to pay for the room as well as the damages that had been done to it, totaling sixteen hundred and fifty dollars. She looked at Lee when he started cursing.

"For that much money, we can replace all our shit." He reminded her that their extra cash was in the luggage. "Mother fuck balls, Lee. Now what do we do? We'll need money to get to them girls. After that, we'll be home free. This is really starting to piss me off with all these extra costs. If I didn't know any better, I'd say that Carter were doing this to us. I know, I know what you're going to say. There ain't any way that she could know that we're coming. But something is slowing us down, and I don't like it."

The uneasy feeling that she'd had yesterday morning returned. Hazel didn't know what had caused it, the last time or this one, but it was something that made her head spin a little as well as her belly lurch. Her momma would have said that she'd stepped onto her own grave. But Hazel wasn't that superstitious. Instead, she thought that it was the uneasy feeling that maybe things were not going as perfectly as they'd hoped they would. She looked over at Lee when he started talking.

"They got us over a barrel with this. We need to get going, but we can't go without the money. And the money is where our luggage is. They want money, and in order for me to get it and pay them for it, I'm going to have to show them where our cash stash is. I don't like that at all. Mother fuck, this is some messed up business we got going here." She said that she was sorry it was coming to this. "Yeah, not your fault. I should have had you stay here until I got back. Then we'd be all right now. Live and learn. I just console myself with knowing that when this is done, we'll have all the money and luggage that we need. And then some."

Lee went into the front office while she stayed behind.

They had been heading out west, where she knew that Rachel lived. But somehow the two of them had ended up in Ohio, and that was even closer than they'd been thinking that they'd have to travel. Like an omen, she thought, and smiled.

It took him nearly an hour to get the situation taken care of. He'd had to prove that the money was in the luggage so that they'd let him open it. It was a nightmare, but at least they were on their way now. And good riddance to this little town.

They were perhaps fifteen hours from Ohio when they finally pulled over for the night. They thought about just staying in their car for their last night on the open road, but Lee really wanted a bed, and she could never deny him anything that he wanted. Besides, he'd been doing all the driving, so she paid for a room for one night, and they were settled in by the time the pizza was delivered.

"No food fights this time. It was fun, but also costly." She laughed when he did. They really had messed up the room from before. But there wasn't any way that she was going to believe it was sixteen hundred dollars, and said that to Lee. "It matters little now. We've paid it, have our things, and we're nearly there. If we get up really early tomorrow and get on the road, we can be to that place she's staying by supper. Tomorrow, we snatch Rachel and then bring Carter to heel. After that, free sailing."

"Free sailing." Hazel looked at her email that they'd set up just for this business, and saw that she had three emails. After reading the first one, she told Lee what it said. "They want proof that she can do these things before they give us the rest of the money. How the hell do we do that? Other than taking her to them, she's not going to perform for us to record her. I guess we'll have to take her to him and hope that he doesn't try and rip us off."

"You're right about her cooperating enough for us to record her. It's doubtful we could get her to do much of anything other than to come with us because we'll have Rachel at gun point. And that might be difficult." Lee laid back on his bed as soon as he ate the last slice of pizza. "I've not even thought of how we get her to them. We should have gotten us a van or something with a cage in the back to keep her out of our way. Damn it. How about we tell him where to come? Once we get Carter, that is. That way he can deal with her on his own."

"I like that idea. That way we have the cash, he has the monster, and we get to take off and find us a little island to buy." That uneasy feeling came over her again. This time she told Lee about it. "It makes me dizzy and my belly churns all up. I don't know what it is, but when I think of this plan, I get that way. Do you suppose Carter is doing this to me? To warn me off from her?"

"I bet it's just heartburn. Did you eat the last time before you got that way?" She told him she didn't remember. "I'm betting that's it. We just had some spicy pizza, and that's all it is. No worries on this. We have this in the bag, love. You'll see. We'll have no trouble. Did you hear from the other party that we were dealing with?"

"They're going to pass on it. Assholes. I could have been talking to someone else by now." She looked at the last email and frowned. "It's from Rachel. Why would she be emailing me after all this time? And for that matter, how did she get our email address?"

"I don't know. Perhaps she wants to get in on this too.

No, that can't be it. She doesn't know what we're doing just yet. See what she has to say, and I'm going to close my eyes." Hazel read over the short email, then read it twice more before she wanted to be sick. Running to the bathroom, she threw up all her dinner and gagged several times before she was able to answer Lee. "What did she say? Christ, you scared me to death the way you ran in there."

"It was from Carter. She said that we'd better have our wills made out properly, because once we come there, we're going to be dead." Her belly churned again, worse than it had before. "Oh Lee, how did she find out? And why would she say something like that to us? We're her parents—she can't kill us."

"Well, she seems to think so." He read over the missive before he looked at her again. "Were you planning to answer her?"

"I wouldn't even know what to say to her. I mean, she just threatened us. Is she allowed to do that after just getting out of prison?" He said that the charges were dropped against her. So it was like she'd done nothing wrong. "Still, there is no cause for her to be going on like that. Doesn't she realize how scary that is? I would turn her into the police if I knew anyone there. That's just not right. And when we get her, I'm going to tell her that too."

"I'm going to email her back and let her know how she made you feel." He started typing. "I'm telling you right now, Hazel, that girl is going to regret messing with you. I'm going to make sure she understands that I'm the boss of her no matter how old she gets. And she'd better remember that too. Damned girls. I wish we'd never had either of them. Of course, we'd not be basking in money soon, but they're no kids of mine if they mess with you."

Hazel read it over before he sent it and felt better than before for them taking a stand. Lee was right, there wasn't any cause at all for her to be saying those things to her. Not at all. And the sooner she got her head on right, the better it would be for her. Hazel was just glad that when this was over, she'd not have to think about her anymore. Either of them.

After getting her shower and laying out her clothing for in the morning, she went to bed. Tomorrow they'd have this thing over with, and then Carter would be out of their hands. And Rachel would more than likely be dead if she had anything to do with it. The girls had been up her ass about one thing or another for years. And having Carter arrested for the robbery had been her biggest joy. But now she was out, and things could go badly for her and Lee. But she wasn't going to think of that right now. She was going to think positively from now on when it came to coming out on top with this.

~~~

Josh read the email three times before he just couldn't sit any more, he had been laughing so hard. "They actually threatened to ground you for telling them to back off? How stupid are these people?"

"What I got a kick out of was how I made my mother sick by saying such hateful things to her, and I should be ashamed of myself." Carter was laughing too, having been in on the fun that they'd been having since yesterday afternoon. "They're planning on selling me off to the highest bidder, and I'm a terrible person for threatening them. Yes, they are pretty stupid. And the fact that they still think they can control me makes me ill."

Carter looked over at Dylan and thanked her again for

getting the email address. "It was my pleasure. And I've gotten permission from my boss to tell you how I got it. We're the one that she's selling you to. Or at least one of them. We've backed out for now, but in a couple of hours we're going to say that we've changed our mind and will be doubling our price for you, Carter. That is, if they can get here to get you. They've run into more problems again. Poor people, they can't seem to catch a break, it seems. This should get them in a tizzy, and those kind of emotions usually mean they'll fuck up."

"I don't understand what they're doing wrong. I mean, other than selling off my sister. But you'd think they'd wonder how they were going to do that if she's able to do the things that she can." Josh nodded at Rachel's question; he had been wondering the same thing. It wasn't as if she was this weakling or something. She was a powerful being. "What can you arrest them for if they just take their daughter with them when they leave? I'm not saying that either of us will go with them, but what is it that they've done to anyone here?"

"They're dealing in human trafficking for one thing. And here is the list of things that we were told that Carter can do. They think that she can move smaller things, nothing as big as the truck she lifted, several times. They said she can also make things fly. I'm assuming that stems from her lifting something up, but I could be wrong." Carter pointed out that she'd only been a teenager when they'd seen her last. "That's what we're hoping for. They don't know you anymore. Also, they don't mention you being able to read something once you touch it. Nor do they say anything about you being able to see into the future. Henry and I think that with you being stronger than you were before, they'll be so surprised that they'll make mistakes. And so far, they've made several."

Rachel asked what they thought was going to happen when they arrived. He knew the answer to this one, he thought, and answered for Dylan. She told him he was more than likely right on that too.

"Kidnap me? Oh, I see—they think that'll make Carter do what they want. And then what do you suppose they'll do with me once they have her? If they get her." No one answered, and Josh wasn't ready to tell his new sister-in-law the answer to that question. "Tell me. I have a feeling that I'm not going to like it."

"They're going to kill you. No witnesses." Rachel looked at Carter as she continued to explain what they all thought was going to happen. "They'll not want to leave any witnesses behind, is my thinking. And having you dead and me gone means that there isn't anyone that knows about the robbery and that they'd done it. Because of the fact that we're close, they'll assume that I told you what really happened, even though I didn't tell you anything. You figured that out on your own."

"You only said that you hadn't robbed the bank." Carter said that she hadn't. "No, I knew that from the start. But how did they do it? I mean, doesn't robbing a bank require some skill at it? That's what I think anyway."

"It does require skill. And we think this wasn't their first robbery. There are three bank robberies that we can assume that they committed. But this last one, there was an off-duty police officer in the bank and he drew on one of them." Dylan handed them a picture of the officer as she continued. "Your father shot him in the head when the shot that he took hit your mother in the arm. It wasn't a wound that stopped her for long, but we found their DNA on the money that they'd

96

left behind."

"Why didn't anyone look at that before they put my sister in prison?" No one answered her, but Josh had a pretty good idea. And when Dylan told her why, he was right.

"They were not there to take the hit, and your sister was a close enough match to your mom that they just went with it. Even though witnesses said that the couple that robbed the bank was older, more mature, they arrested Carter and closed the book on the robbery. It was more convenient for them to have her arrested than to let the robbery go unsolved. Their way, insurance claims could be made. The man that was killed, his family was also compensated by the bank's insurance." Rachel said it was unfair, and Dylan shrugged and continued. "I'm sure that it happens a great deal. Not like this was run through, but it happens."

Carter began to pace, and when she suddenly stopped, Josh stood up. She'd been nervous all day, and it wasn't until a few hours ago that she told them that they'd be there tonight. That was why they were all at Evan's house, so that they could be protected by Dylan and her men. Sunny was pissy about not being able to help, but they didn't want the baby hurt. She said that she'd get over it, but she wasn't all that thrilled with being left out of it all. Josh had to laugh every time he thought of Sunny trying to look all mean, when all he could see was a maternal woman with a big belly.

"They just crossed over the state line to here." Dylan sent two of her men out to make the phone calls. Josh wasn't sure what they could be about, but he knew they were safe in her hands. "I've been thinking about this for a couple of hours now. I think I'd like to deal with them before they try and take Rachel."

"How would you deal with them?" Josh had a feeling he knew the answer, but he wanted to hear it from her. "You can't kill them, if that's what you're thinking. That would haunt you for a very long time."

"No it wouldn't. They've not been a part of my life since before I left home. And I have no love for either of them. Spending all that time in prison, it gave me time to think and reflect on what they've done to me and why. I don't have anything for either of them. No love, no respect. Nothing. To me, they might as well be strangers. But, I'm not going to kill them. Unless it comes to them hurting my sister — then all bets are off." Josh asked her what her plan was. "I will show them what I am. All of me."

No one said anything, but he could tell they were all thinking how bad that could be too. Only he knew that she and him could sort of travel together, and what they could do while someplace else. There were other things that she could do as well that no one had known about but him now.

Carter could manipulate memory, yes. But she could also make it so that they could see things that weren't there, as well as hurt when she told them to. But the scariest thing that she did, at least to him, was that she could throw balls of fire, as many as she wanted. Like she had an endless supply of them. He was sure that she did too.

He had told Dylan about the ropes and chains that the Comptons had purchased. He only said that Carter knew that they'd gotten them. Carter had told him that her parents knew the things were missing, but didn't say much about it. Josh also mentioned guns, but they no longer had them. Josh thought that Dylan might have an idea that he was stretching the truth a little, but she didn't ask, and he didn't say any more. Instead, they all knew that now they were without the basic equipment that was needed to kidnap and hold someone against their will.

"And when you show them your all, what do you think is going to happen then? I have no problem at all with you killing them both—they're more than likely going to be spending a great deal of time, if not life, in prison anyway. What is it you're hoping will happen by you showing them what you can do?" At Dylan's question, Carter looked at him and he nodded, telling her that he was with her every step of the way. "Carter?"

"Rape their mind and erase every bit of knowledge of Rachel and me. Let them think that they've been on this mission of theirs all along on information that they've read in one of those magazines at the end of the grocery aisle." Dylan asked her what that would do. "Hopefully drive them insane, where they'll need to be locked up for the rest of their days. I don't trust the prison system. I was there for ten years, and I know firsthand what can happen to them. Nothing. All the stories that you see on television are, for the most part, untrue. I want them to suffer. And badly."

Rachel cleared her throat, and everyone turned to look at her. Josh was afraid that she wasn't going to like this idea and try to talk Carter out of it. But when she stood up and went to Carter, hugging her tightly, he watched the two of them.

"Kill them or make them insane, I don't care anymore. But if they hurt you again, I swear to you, Carter, I will hunt them down and do as much damage as my puny little body can do to them." Carter told her that she loved her. "And I love you. I'm so glad that you found Josh through all this. He's made you almost the sister that you used to be. Almost.

You still have some way to go, but I love having you back any way I can get you."

Dylan laughed before speaking. "All right, you handle them. But know this—if it gets out of hand, I go in with guns blazing. Just like a rabid dog, they need to be put down and out of their—or in this case, our—misery." Josh held onto Carter when Dylan spoke. "You will be careful, won't you?"

"Yes. I won't let them take Rachel either. If they do, they'll die. That's why I want to do it when they arrive." Carter frowned. "How do they know where we are, anyway?"

"That would be me. And you two will need to get married today too. If not today then very soon. It's all arranged. The announcement is in the paper as of today, and it says in the article that the two of you will be residing in this town. After that, it's a piece of cake to find out where you'll be living. You don't get to live in a small town like this and be able to keep a secret like this." Josh asked her who was going to talk about it. "Why, your grandda, of course. He's all up for having a little fun with this, so long as he stays safe. I told him if he gets hurt even a little, I was going to beat his ass until he said uncle. I love that old man, and he's the best there is."

Josh had to agree. Grandda was a good man, and he'd do this up right too. Mom and Dad, they'd be helping too, he'd bet, and as soon as the Comptons arrived in town, things would start to go a little easier for them all. This wouldn't be hanging over their head all the time.

Chapter 7

Waldo bought the land that was next to the property that he really wanted. Everybody was paid up but one, and he wasn't going to come on the hunt. Something about nightmares that he was dealing with. Whatever—he didn't get his deposit back, and that was final. He looked over the spread-out map as he tried to think what he had to do next. He had to get himself a couple of people that they could chase and kill, first of all.

That was proving harder than he'd thought it should be. There were, when he'd first arrived here, several people that looked to be homeless and hanging out at the shelter. Waldo had paid a guy twenty bucks for him to give Waldo a good counting of how many people stayed at the shelter any given night. As well as finding out if there were any that didn't go inside and use it, opting to hang out outside.

There were currently twenty that stayed at the shelter for the most part. Some nights one or two of them wouldn't show up before the doors were locked, and they'd have to find a place to stay elsewhere. And the man had told him that those were the only ones that didn't stay there. If you were locked out for some reason, then that was the only others he knew about. As for names, Waldo couldn't give him enough money, he'd said, to get those.

"They like their privacy just like everybody else." Waldo thought that was the funniest thing he'd heard in a while. Homeless people who wanted their privacy. But he wasn't worried; he'd find one or two of them while they were out during the day, and take them to the barn that was on his newly purchased land.

He had four men that were going to go on the first hunt during the daylight hours, and three for the night one. They had paid more for the privilege of hunting at night. Some people were just too easy to please. Except for Joshua Whitfield.

The kid would not sell him the land. It wasn't as if he couldn't have his pick of his daddy's property. The family owned nearly ten thousand acres that spread out over three states. The house would have been something that he would have lived in between hunting trips too. Now they were all cozied up in it, and burrowed in like a tick on a dog.

The only thing that he could think to do was to burn them out. And that posed more problems than he wanted to deal with right now. If he wasn't so pressed for time, he'd have done it, but he had a hunting trip scheduled for two weeks and still not enough land to have fun on.

Waldo was thinking about just using the Whitfield land; it wasn't as if he couldn't monitor the entire area, especially from his place of business in town. But that would embarrass him should he get caught, and he didn't want to look the fool in front of his clients.

Waldo looked over at the urn that held his good buddy, Tommy. The police had found no reason to believe that he'd been murdered. It took him the better part of a day to figure out that someone had messed with their minds. All they saw was a drunk young man had fallen coming up the steps to his house and had busted his head open, thus killing him. None of them had seen the bones at the back of his neck. Not seen the amount of blood that had stained his front stoop. Nor did any of them say anything about the fact that his belly had been sliced open and his guts had fallen out. He'd only seen that when they'd picked him up to put him in the ambulance. Whoever this vampire was, he had really done a number on everyone to keep his handiwork quiet.

He missed Tommy. Daily he would think of something and want to run it past him. But some asshole had killed him, and he still didn't have any idea why. Oh sure, he'd been warned by him to stop with all his plans, but what was he supposed to do now? He had things all lined up, and if he was honest with himself, he didn't want to quit. This was going to make him a great deal of money. Money that he'd already spent.

It had been stupid, now that he thought about it, to use some of his money to put a deposit down on an island. But it had been going too cheap for him to not take the deal. The couple that sold it to him said that it wasn't the same anymore. Not with the ships going by it all the time. And the helicopter that they had, the one to get back and forth to the island, wasn't up to par. That was something that they said to him several times—he'd need to purchase a new chopper to get back and forth.

Tommy had been shocked by his plan when he'd heard about it. "You've never seen the island, yet you plopped down a million and a half dollars? For all you know it could be covered in some man-eating plants that will likely kill you the first time that you go there." He told him he'd seen the pictures of it. "Well, then that makes it all right, doesn't it? You've seen pictures. I have pictures of people in my wallet that I don't have a clue who they are, so that people will think I have family. But they're not real. This is a scam, I know it."

So, he had rented a helicopter and had the couple take him to it. They couldn't land, he forgot the reason why, but he was excited to see no man-eating plants and a beautiful home that looked like it had several hundred bedrooms—not really, but it was huge. So, he'd been happy, but Tommy had still been skeptical.

Today he was going to pay off the island and the couple would give him the keys and the deed. He was so fucking excited about that, he nearly forgot that he had other work to do today as well. The land was going to mess him up.

The kid, Whitfield, had been so unfriendly when he'd gone by to see him that first day. And since then as well. Three times Waldo had sent him a registered letter, and all three times it had come back to him, refused. He'd have to go talk to him. Or better yet, he'd have his attorney go and talk to him. That would probably scare the shit out of the kid, that an attorney was coming to see him, and he'd give in. That's what he was hoping for anyway.

At noon, he made his way into town. He needed to go by the bank to meet the couple. He wished now that he'd written down their names. It was as if he had a mental block about it. But as soon as he walked into the big imposing building, he

104

could see them right where they said they'd be. And within an hour, he not only had the keys—a massive amount of them, he thought—but the deed as well.

Waldo loved the fact that there wasn't an address on the paperwork. A longitude and latitude was all he had in order to get to his place. Opening a post office box had been the next thing on his list of things that he had to do. Waldo thanked the couple for reminding him to do so.

And he now knew their names. Kent and Sara Shaft. He had no idea why that sort of name would have eluded him, but now he had it on his paperwork and he was set to go. Tommy would have no doubt thought that it was an omen to have names like that. Waldo got a chuckle out of it as he finished up at the post office. He was an official homeowner.

His next stop was his attorney. They were meeting for lunch at the bistro on Tenth. He so loved their thick sandwiches that they made there. And his favorite was a roast beef on rye with all the trimmings. As he waited for his food, he told Reeve Winters what he wanted done.

"You do know that this family could easily buy and sell you several times over, don't you? They've been rich since I think money was invented. And they have no problem sharing it, either. They've done a lot for that little town." He said that he only wanted to buy the land, not get into bed with them. "All right, I'll do this, but I'd not expect too much to come from it. These people get what they want and do what they want, but nobody gets hurt with it. What do you want it so bad for, anyway?"

"I have some people coming into town that want to do a bit of hunting. When I was out walking about, I accidently got onto his property and saw the amount of deer and other animals there that we could make a meal of." Sure, he thought to himself. But no humans, which was what he really wanted. "It's a nice piece of land out there. You should see it."

"I've been to the Whitfield ranch a few times. They have the best Fourth of July picnic you've ever been too. I'm telling you, Waldo, getting in bad with these people will have consequences. And none of them good." He repeated that it was just land he wanted to buy. "I'll go and talk to Josh today. I heard he's just about to tie the knot with a nice young woman. Nice to see them boys getting married. They're a good group."

He'd heard it all before from the townspeople. The Whitfields were like gods to them. And none of them were mean or nasty about helping a fellow out either. Waldo had even heard that they made loans to people that needed them and didn't hound them when they were a little late. All he could think about with them was that they were saps, every one of them.

After his lunch he headed towards his next destination. His list was being ticked off much faster than he could have hoped for. Waldo only had one more stop to make, and he didn't anticipate any issues there either. He had to secure places for the men to stay, and the little town actually had three bed and breakfasts that were right in town.

"I'm sorry, sir, but we're booked up for those dates. Most of the town is." He asked her what was going on. "Well, we have this convention that comes in once a year. It's a big deal around here. I'm surprised that you've not heard all the talk about it. Why, most of these shops are in the red deeply before that week, then all of a sudden, they're riding down the lane of profit making."

106

"So, there is nothing, anywhere? How do you accommodate people that just come in to town for the afternoon and decide to stay?" She said that she'd tell them the same as she had him, they were booked up. "This is just ridiculous. I've had this planned for months now, and you're telling me that you can't accommodate a few people coming in? I suppose I should have called you up right when I had it all arranged that they were coming, two months ago."

"Wouldn't have done you any good. I've had these reservations since last year. You see, I'm right here on the main drag of the town, and they can just pop on by here and drop off whatever they buy. I'm convenient, you might say." He wanted to punch her in her convenient mouth, is what he wanted to do. "And you can go to the other places in town, but it won't do you much good. Just like me, they'll be all booked up as well. It's a big deal to this town."

So were his plans to him, but he didn't tell her that. She'd just go on again how this was a money maker for her and shit on him. He would have to call the other hotels that were in the next town over and put them up there. Then he'd have to rent a car or two for them to get back and forth. Not that he wasn't making a profit from this already, but shit like this was eating into his money. And he didn't care for it.

Waldo had no more luck with the hotels than he had the B&Bs. They too were booked up, and he thought if one more person told him how this was benefiting them, he might take a gun out and shoot them all. As it stood right now, he had nowhere for the men that were coming to stay. And so far, there were no restaurants that weren't booked up solid for reservations.

What the hell was this thing that booked so many people

to come to a one stop light area and had the entire town at their beck and call? He started to ask the woman that he was talking to, but she hung up on him. He wanted to tell himself that they'd lost the connection, his cell service was shit out here, but he was in a pissy mood and that's what he was going with.

Waldo wasn't sure what he could do now. Other than to shove them into his rental, he didn't have any idea where he was supposed to put all the people that he had coming. And then figure out how to feed them as well.

~~~

Josh asked Reeve why the man was wanting his land. "I mean, it's not like he has anything around here that would hold him to this area. Why my land?"

"I believe that he just purchased the land to the east of yours. I think it only comes to about nine acres. Maybe a little less. But he claims that he just wants to hunt, and there is prime area around where you have your home." Josh knew just what he was looking to do, and didn't care for him bringing this man in on it. "He told me to tell you that he's willing to pay just about any price that you wish, and buy the house from you as well."

"Mr. Winters, you're a nice man, but I don't think you have all the facts with this deal he's got you chasing. You know my sister-in-law, Dylan. She's coming by here to tell you what she's found out." He asked if it was about the land. "Yes, my land, as well as some of the things that she's been able to dig up on this man. Most of it isn't showing him in a good light."

Dylan showed up with Evan and they all sat in his office, talking. Carter joined them a few minutes later and had some tea and coffee brought in. He was trying to convert her over to tea, but she wasn't having it.

"Eight years ago, there was a big to do over hunting on a large piece of land that didn't belong to the man who had set it up. Back then, Waldo Moody was going by the name of Chester Wine. He's had a couple of other names that he's gone by, but his real name is Waldo Chester. Anyway, the land in question didn't belong to him, but he'd had wild animals brought in that were going to be used for a hunt. Men and women paid several thousand dollars to hunt what turned out to be endangered species." She handed him photographs of Waldo, then and now. "As you can see there, it's the same man."

"Yes, but he never said anything about bringing in animals. What he told me was that there were deer and other animals on the property that he wanted to hunt." Josh asked him if he knew that they let other shifters on the land. "No. Well, now that you mention it, I should have known. But no, I didn't think about that. You think that he's seen them there and that's what he's going after?"

"No, he's got bigger game in mind." Reeve looked at Carter when she spoke. "He has it in his head to hunt humans. He's already made inquiries at the local shelter to pick off a few of the people there to use for his hunting buddies."

"You mean he's actually going to be hunting some of the people from the shelter?" Reeve was so shocked his voice had gone up a couple of notches. "You must have it wrong, young lady. There is..... Why, that's terrible. I mean, I thought it was horrible of him to want to hunt the shifters on the land, but this...this makes it so much worse. Has he done this before?"

Dylan handed him the picture that she'd shown Josh last

night. They were planning to go to the police about this today, but when Waldo had sent his attorney over, Dylan thought it a good idea to get it going this way as well. The picture was of three men, one of them Waldo, standing next to a dead body. The man that they all assumed had killed the younger man held his head up like he was so proud of the bullet hole in his forehead.

"Where did you get this?" Dylan told him that she was able to find it on the dark web. "Yes, well, I would imagine that you'd not want this out where just anyone could find it. And you're sure that this man was killed like this? Not that I doubt you, Mrs. Whitfield, but this is just too horrific for words for me."

"Yes, it's on his web page that talks about big hunts and unusual game. We're thinking that he means humans again. That man there paid over five thousand dollars to go on this hunt with Waldo. And when it was done, he took one of the fingers of that man home with him." Reeve looked slightly ill. "Two months ago, he had a flurry of activity at his bank where deposits were coming in to go on the expedition of a lifetime. He wants Josh's land because it's far enough off the beaten path that no one would suspect what's going on there, and the house gives it the appearance of being just that, a homestead. The fucker is going to run his home like a bed and breakfast, we think, and keep it more quiet than before."

"I just don't know what to say. I've only been his attorney for the last year or so. I knew that he was into some strange things, but never anything like this." He looked at all of them, then at Josh. "Josh, you have no idea how sorry I am that I'm a part of this. I didn't know what he was up to. I swear to you on my children's hearts I didn't."

110

"I didn't think you did. But something must be done about him, and soon. If what he's said in town about having guests coming in is true, this thing is set to happen in about two weeks. I haven't any idea what he hopes to accomplish with this other than a shit load of money. How did he not think that someone would have known what he was doing?" Josh looked at Carter when she suddenly stiffened. "Are you all right?"

Nodding, she told him that she'd tell him later. He had a feeling that her parents were closer than she'd thought. Great, first Waldo and now her parents. Josh wanted to put them all in jail and be done with them, but he also knew that things had to work out the way they were in order to catch all parties that were involved. In the case of her parents, there was another buyer out there that they didn't know.

"I'd like to work with you on this. I'm not sure what I can do, but you ask, and I'll do my best to get it for you." Josh looked at Reeve when he spoke. "I can't tell you enough how sorry and embarrassed I am about this. Your family has always been good to mine, and I hate that he's brought me into this in a bad light. I'm still having trouble wrapping my mind around this, but I don't doubt that he's as guilty as sin."

Dylan started to tell him what she had as a plan. It was simple really. Once they all showed up at the property, then her team would come in and arrest them. Josh knew that things could and more than likely would go wrong, but the way she had it planned out, it was going to net them the most people for this going down. And Josh wanted it over with. Reaching out to Carter, he asked her if she was all right.

Yes. As you have guessed, they're in the next town over in a hotel. They've taken a suite so that they can hide things in the room

111

that they're going to need. He asked her what that might be. *Guns for one thing. They have also purchased chains to hold me with. I wonder if they realize that simple chains will not hold me. I guess they'll figure it out soon, but it's stupid all the same.*

I'm so sorry that you have to go through with this. But at least you know that Rachel is going to be safe and that I'll not let anyone hurt you. He laughed a little. *Of course, you're much stronger and more capable of keeping us both safe, but I had to say that.*

Of course you did. And I love you for it. He knew there was going to be a "but," and he wasn't surprised when she said the rest of what she was thinking. *But they're not coming here for any other reason than to kill Rachel and to take me someplace where someone can cut me up and run copious numbers of tests on me. How could someone do that to their own flesh and blood? I mean, to kill Rachel as if she were nothing more than something in their way and be so callous about it, it boggles my mind.*

I know that it would me as well. And you're right, they're callous and cold-hearted bastards. And when they come here, which I'm assuming will be soon, then we'll deal with them in the same manner. They're going to be in for a huge surprise if they think that we're going to just roll over and let them take what they want. She told him that she knew that as well. *We've got this, babe. You and the rest of my family, we're going to come out on top, see if we don't.*

And this idiot — what do we do about him? He's trying to take our home from us. And I like our house. He did as well and told her that they were working with the best and it would all resolve itself. *I hope so. I'd hate to go after him on my own. He won't care for the way things go. I'll take him out in a heartbeat.*

It wasn't a threat, but a promise he could hear in her voice. This guy was going to be toast as soon as he crossed the line. And Josh knew that the guy was going to do that sooner rather than later. Honestly, he couldn't wait to have one less thing to worry about. There was too much going on in their lives right now to have some guy trying to buy up land to kill other human beings on.

"Well, I can tell you this, I'm finished with him as an attorney." Dylan cautioned him about being too rash. "You think he might kill me? Well, he can try. I don't pussyfoot around when it comes to being an upstanding person. You can take that to the bank, my dear."

"I would hope that you don't say anything to him just yet." Reeve nodded, saying he understood. "Yes, and I hope you'll understand that I'd rather you didn't quit him just yet. I need to get all the men in one place to finish this. They're hiring a man to help them murder someone. That is against the law as well."

"I can understand that, I can. What do I tell him about young Josh here? I can't give him the real reason for him not selling." Dylan said that she had a plan for that as well, and told him. "Ah yes, I see—Josh and his lovely bride are on their honeymoon for a month. Yes, I can see all kinds of ways that will help you. He might just trespass again, and that's something else that you can add to his bad deeds."

All they had to do was lay low for a couple of weeks. Josh could think of all kinds of things he could be occupying his mind with while laying low. Making love to his future wife was one of them. And having sex with her was a good second too. Smiling, he looked over at Carter when he realized, again, how much he loved this woman, and was glad that she'd come into his life when she had.

Chapter 8

Adrian looked over the notes that Dylan had brought him. There was a lot to be thankful for when you had someone like her in your corner. When he asked her if this was correct, she just gave him the look that he'd come to start calling "Are you fucking kidding me right now?"

"So, these people that are coming have sold off their daughter to the highest bidder, and are going to stiff the buyer because you're the one that bid more? How do you find this shit? I mean, is there a direct link to a site that is call henchmen and assholes?" She glared at him this time. "Look, it's not that I don't believe you—I really do—but this shit is just out there. Where would they have even begun to find this person that they're selling her to?"

"There are all kinds of sites for anything and everything you want. And we have a team of people that all they do all day is look for sites like this one. Then there is another team that joins these sites, so they can be aware of any changes that may or may not take place within it. You'd be surprised what

I can tell you happens just in this state. You'd be a graying old man in about ten minutes."

"Don't tell me, please. I'd like to live in the dark about it for the rest of my life, if possible. So, they figured out who they could get to pay them a great deal of money for Carter. And they're probably going to use Josh or Rachel as bait to do it." Dylan told him they were using one of them as an illusion to get Carter. "I don't understand then. What's the difference?"

"They'll kill whoever they take as soon as they take them. They, first of all, won't want to mess with them by keeping them around tied up. And secondly, no witnesses. That's what I'd do if I was the one selling off my relatives. But I would have been a good deal smarter about it." He asked her what she'd have done. "Rachel might have been the key in their book, but Josh is a much better target. But I wouldn't have bothered with him at all. I'd not take him out, though, until I had her. That way if she demanded to speak to him, then she could without any shit going on about faking it."

"Christ, remind me to never have you tell me shit like this again." She laughed, and he smiled with her. She might be ruthless and a killer, but she was also his family and he loved her very much. Like his sister. "So, what is it you want me to do? I'm assuming this is something that is going to get the voters to love me even more. By the way, I'm a little nervous about all this shit I'm supposed to be taking care of. Whatever will I do once I'm in office and there is nothing else going on?"

"You'll have plenty to do, trust me. I could tell you several things right now that you could be working on and never see the end of it." He told her again, he didn't want to know. "Party pooper. But you are going to be instrumental in taking this guy down. And having the men with him arrested.

Also, we're going to play up the fact that you knew that the Comptons were coming and what their plans were concerning Carter. I'm afraid that one is going to require your attention first. They arrived in Columbus last night, and have taken a hotel room."

"Will anyone be hurt? I mean, are we killing them right off or are we going to have them arrested?" She told him that she was hoping for death but was more than likely going to have to arrest them. "But you're waiting on the last part of the puzzle, aren't you?"

"Yes, I don't know who the person is that they've made arrangements with to have Carter sold. He's out there, thinking that this is going to be easy, and I'm worried about him starting up some kind of lab or something that will have Carter as the main attraction." Adrian asked Dylan if Carter was all right with him being the heavy in all this. "Yes, it was actually her idea. She wants to stay out of the light as much as possible with this now. I know that before she wanted to go ahead and confront them, but she's decided that it wouldn't such a good idea. What if they got away, is her thinking. We're going to portray her as this shy little backward woman who was unfairly sentenced to a decade of her life in prison. All because of her parents. Then when the public finds out that they're also the ones that were going to sell her off to the highest bidder for some insane reason, that will get her out of the limelight and put her parents and this other person front and center."

"And you think this plan of yours will work? Both of them?" She said that she hoped so. "I do as well. Just tell me what you want and I'm there for you. On both accounts. Oh, I also wanted to thank you for the downtown office. Lily is in seventh heaven arranging for my campaign for this governor seat that she says I'm a shoo in for."

"You are. Henry is going to come out and pose with you a few times, to commend you for things that you've done here in the name of progress. He also said to tell you that when you do put your name in the hat for governor, he wants you to call him direct. He said that the newspapers will have fun with that one." Adrian nodded; that was still months away. "It'll come up on you quicker than you think it will. Just be prepared for anything and everything that someone tosses at you. And I'll make sure that you get things finished with these people too."

After she left him to set things up, he looked over the paperwork that she'd given him again. Henry was shuffling things through her that he wanted him to have. There was a lot of it too. And just today, he'd sent him a proposal for him to look over that Congress wanted to put through. It was one of his ideas on how to keep kids in school when the dropout rate had been rising in his state.

It was almost so simple that Adrian didn't think it would work. Just give them a bonus, in the form of a scholarship, if they managed to stay in school and make the grades that were high enough to ensure that they'd be able to get through college without much trouble. There was also a similar program for those that were doing well enough in school to go to college, but might not have either the money or other means to make it happen. His brothers were helping with that as well. Evan was even donating some of his free time in order to help kids fill out resumes, as well as applications for grants and such.

When he looked up from the paperwork when his eyes

started to get blurry, he was surprised to find his grandda there. He'd been there a while too, if the newspaper he was quietly reading was any indication. He was on page ten of it. Adrian asked him how long he'd been there.

"Not long. Well, about twenty minutes. You sure were studying that paper there like you was going to have a test on it later. Are you?" He told him what it was. "Well, ain't that something? My grandboy is helping the president out with a project. You sure do make this old man proud."

"I'm proud of you as well, Grandda. It's good to see you feeling better." He said that he still had some hard days, but there was so much to do now that he didn't want to miss anything. "I can understand that. I still find myself thinking about Grandma and what she'd be thinking about this or that. She'd be proud of all of us, wouldn't she? The kids coming along would also thrill her. I heard that you and Evan's two boys were fishing this morning. Catch anything?"

"We don't go for catching anything. It's a time for us to be manly men. I'm not sure that little Kyle gets it yet, but he sure does have a lot of questions, don't he?" Adrian laughed and said that he'd heard that as well. "I came by to see if you wanted to grab some dinner with me. Your mom and dad are going to have them a good dinner out, just the two of them. I don't think they've had much time to do that while raising you boys up."

"No, it's doubtful that they did. Yes, I'd love to have dinner with you. But I'm sort of on call with Dylan. She has this plan going on that she wants me to be a part of. So, if she calls, I have to go to her." Grandda said that he understood that. "Wonderful. What did you have in mind?"

They ended up at the little diner that was doing a hell

119

of a business. People were out and about, enjoying the nice weather that they were having. Fall was only a short few weeks away, and while it was nice today, tomorrow was supposed to be cold and wet. Grandda ordered after he did, and Adrian asked him what he wanted.

"Want? I don't want anything but to have dinner with my new mayor." Adrian just cocked a brow at him. "All right, durn kids. I just want something to do. Everybody around here seems to have a job or something, and here I am just about to bust because there doesn't seem to be jack butts for me to get into."

"I thought you and the boys were hanging out." He said that they were getting ready for Thanksgiving pageants and the what for. "So you're lonely. I never thought I'd say this, but you need to get a job. Not just something that you can hang out at once in a while, but something that keeps you busy every day. Otherwise you're going to become a pain in the bottom and no one will want you around."

"You don't think I don't already know that? Even my darling Eve, she told me just yesterday that I had to get out from under her feet. All I was doing was trying to help her with jelly making. You'd of thought that I was taking spoonfuls of it instead of an occasional bite of it." Adrian laughed. "It ain't funny, son. I'm bored out of my mind, and I think if I suggest fishing once more to those great grandboys of mine, they're going to rebel."

"Mr. Whitfield, did you say you were looking for a job?" Shirley Mason, the owner and operator of the Mason Jar Servings, looked like she was on her last legs right now. "If you can make coffee and run the cash register, you have a job. I can't do that counter and wait on people too. And my

120

hubby, he said he's not touching that contraption."

"Really?" She told him how much she'd paid him an hour, and she'd even feed him when he worked. "You got yourself a deal. Let me eat my dinner with Adrian here and I'll run the register. You might have to show me how a bit, but I've done it before."

By the time their dinners arrived, Grandda had the register down pat. He was running to the counter to make coffee between bites. Even Adrian helped out by pouring coffee when it was needed, and even served up some ice cream when Shirley showed him how to do it. Someone from the newspaper had come in to eat dinner, and took some snaps of him and the rest of the crew helping out a friend. Adrian was having as much fun as his grandda was.

When the rush slowed down, he finished his meal and then had a piece of apple pie for dessert. Shirley wanted to give him his meal too, but he told her that he'd not do that to her. She was making a living and he didn't mind helping out. He also told her how much fun he'd had working with his grandda.

"The two of you saved my butt tonight. I had a waitress quit on me, and after she quit without giving me any kind of notice and the other girl that works for me just couldn't come in. I don't suppose you know anybody that is looking for a crappy job where the pay sucks, do you?" He told her that he'd look around. "I'd appreciate that. It's been hard these last few weeks with the kids home from college and all."

When Rachel showed up with Dylan to have a bite to eat too, he was telling them that Grandda had a job and that Shirley was looking for help. Rachel said she'd do it. He wasn't sure if she was serious or not, and asked her.

"Oh yes, I'm used to working long hard hours, and I used to wait tables to work my way through college. This would be nice for me. I need to get a job anyway, and this would be perfect." He told her where to find Shirley, and when she left he looked at Dylan.

"Evan got called into work for an emergency, and you just took my dinner date away too. I think I should be mad at you, but I just can't bring myself to do it. How's the paperwork going?" He told her that he had read it all today. "Good. I'm expecting the Comptons tomorrow. And I've already spoken to Rachel and Carter. Speaking of which, did you know that she can sort of invade dreams?"

"I don't even know what that means." She explained to him just as it had been explained to her by Josh and Carter. "So, they can even interact with the people, but they don't know that they're there. That sounds...I'm not sure how that sounds, to be honest with you. Creepy, for one thing, and very helpful too. What did she find out when she did her little walk?"

"Her and Josh sort of hang out together when they're doing it. They don't want a lot of people to know it, so mum's the word. But here's the thing that freaks me out a bit—they can touch things and pick them up like they're really there." He asked her what they'd done. "Took the chains and guns out of her parents' trunk, and Josh slashed their tires too. Slowed them down a bit. I think there might have been more done, but they're not talking right now. But you know me, I'll get to the bottom of it."

He did know her well enough to know that. And she'd have every detail worked out as well as all the known names that the bad guys had. She was that good at her job. And she

122

had the resources to do it. Dylan was smart, as well as gifted when it came to snooping things out. And Sunny was running a close second. The two of them were a hell of a duo. But only if they were on your side. Otherwise, you were so fucked.

~~~

Lee couldn't believe his luck when he'd come into town to get a look around and had been told about the new waitress at Mason's. Not that he thought it would be Rachel, but when he'd walked into the place, he could have been knocked over with a feather. Sitting down at the first empty booth he came to, he messaged Hazel to tell her. Then Rachel came to his table.

"What can I get you? The blue plate today is meatloaf with mashed—" He asked her if she knew who he was. "Oh yeah, I know who you are. You're my biological father. I'm assuming that Mother dearest will be coming by later?"

"I just let her know that I found you." She told him she wasn't missing. "I just wanted to come by and see what you were up to."

"You did not. Don't lie to me again. You came by to see if you could take me away and make Carter do things for you. Well, it won't work this time. Carter is her own person, and if she doesn't want to go someplace with you, then no matter who you have in your clutches, she won't go." He was embarrassed at how loud she'd been and looked around. "Don't worry, Daddy dearest, the entire town cares about Carter and me, so you'll have to go through all of them to get me anyplace. Now, do you want to order or not?"

He ordered the first thing he saw on the menu, then she walked away. Lee wasn't sure what to think about this version of Rachel. She used to be so timid and kind. That's why they thought it would be easy to take her and then get Carter. It didn't look like that was going to work.

Hazel messaged him back, telling him to take her. So instead of going over the entire thing with her that he and Rachel had talked about, he called her. After telling her what she'd said and her attitude toward him—hostile, Lee told her—she told him that it wasn't right.

"I know. It's like she's this different person than we knew from before." Hazel asked him what she was doing in the restaurant. "She's waiting tables. And doing a good job of it too. Provided that she doesn't dump my meal on me when it comes back."

"I wish I was there right now, but I will be in a few minutes. Order me whatever you're having." Since he didn't know, he told her that he'd get her the special. "Oh, I've not had meatloaf in ages. Yes, that's good. I should be there in about five or so minutes."

When Rachel brought him the bowl of cole slaw, he told her that Hazel wanted the blue plate. Without a word she walked away, leaving his glass of water behind with his rolls and slaw. After his first bite, he knew that he had died and gone to heaven. It was the best slaw that he'd ever eaten.

By the time Hazel joined him at the table, he'd gotten a glass of tea as well as some more of the rolls that were brought. Hazel's green salad was put down, and Rachel asked her if she wanted tea or coffee.

"You know I don't drink coffee. My goodness, you'd think you don't know me." Rachel said that she didn't any more. "Yes, you do. I'm your mother. I know that it's been a long time, but I know things about you too. You used to be so sweet all the time."

124

"I grew up when you had my sister arrested for a crime that she didn't commit. You'll be happy to know that the police are aware of what went down and are currently looking for you. They're in no hurry, mind you—they have bigger fish to fry." She moved away from the table when one of the other people eating called for her.

"She sure has a terrible way about her. Carter must have told her that we did the robbery or something. That would be the only way she'd know that the police are looking for us." Lee asked her if she was going to eat her rolls. "Yes, I am. You can't just fill up on rolls, Lee. While we don't know if the food is good here or not, which I'm thinking not, then we'll have more rolls. But you can't eat them all."

"I think the food will be terrific. And I'm betting that the dressing on your salad is homemade too. Nothing this good comes from a can." He snatched another roll and buttered it with the creamy mixture that was in a cold crock. "She told me that she's not going to cooperate when we take her. Do you suppose that she'll give us a hard time?"

"Yes. And I don't care. We'll kill her where she stands if she's too much trouble." He finished off his roll when the platters came. And they were platters, not little round plates like he had expected. "Holy shit, Hazel, this is a lot of food. I want to try yours and you can have some of mine."

He had what the menu called baked steak and taters. When Rachel had returned to ask him what sort of vegetable he wanted with his dinner, he'd asked her again what he was having. There was slices of pot roast that looked tender enough to cut with his fork. Green beans with chunks of ham in them. Mashed potatoes that were smothered in dark brown gravy with mushrooms in it. And a side of lima beans too. He looked at Hazel's platter.

There were three big thick slices of the prettiest meatloaf that he'd ever seen. And it had a tomato sauce crust on the top just like he loved it. She had green beans too, and the fluffiest white mashed potatoes. They looked like puffs of clouds on her plate. Before he could reach over and taste her dinner, she was already reaching for his.

They both moaned at the same time. Christ, this was better than good, it was died and gone to heaven good. As they kept sharing each other's food, Rachel set another basket of rolls by their plates and refilled both their drinks. He might have spoken to her again, tried to be friendly so that she'd be all right with going with them when they needed her, but his mouth was full. When he couldn't eat any more, he leaned back on the seat and thought about unbuttoning his pants. They'd gotten uncomfortably tight on him, and he was aching a little.

"Lee, I stand corrected. This was far and away the best meal I've had in a very long time. I mean, even the portions were a good size. Please tell me that this didn't just cost us an arm and a leg." He showed her the bill that had shown up when the food had. "Six dollars and ninety-nine cents for yours, and five ninety-nine for mine? That can't be right. And they didn't charge us for the extra rolls either. You think Rachel is giving us a discount? That would be really nice to know. We can make it back here when she's working for the next couple of days."

"She didn't give us a discount. That's what the menu said they cost." He pulled the one out behind the ketchup and showed her. "See, the blue plate special—that's what you got—is cheaper by a buck when it's the special, I guess. And refills on drinks and rolls are free, it says here."

Rachel came back, and they tried very hard not to look impressed. She took away their empty plates and asked them if they wanted pie. Before he could tell her no, they were much too full, she started naming them off.

"We have peach cobbler and apple dumplings. There is lemon meringue as well as chocolate. Cherry pie, rhubarb pie, strawberry pie that is made with her frozen strawberries, as well as blackberry and blueberry pie." Hazel asked her what she meant by using her frozen strawberries. "The others are made right here with everything fresh. The strawberries are from her garden in the spring, and she froze them to use in pies when they were no longer in season. Which is it you want?"

"I want peach cobbler with ice cream." Rachel asked him if he wanted it warmed up a bit. "Yes, I'd love that. Thanks."

Hazel looked at him like he was insane, but she ordered too. "Lemon meringue for me, and I'll have a cup of tea with the bag on the side. I don't want it too strong."

When Rachel walked away, he looked around. There were perhaps twenty or so people in the place, and they all seemed to be good-natured people. And, they all seemed to like Rachel. One man, who was running the register, seemed to know everyone, and talked to them while they were checking out like he was their long-lost friend. He was the one that brought Hazel her tea.

"You folks should just climb on back in your car and give up this crap you have going on with them girls of yours. I've kinda taken a shine to them, and I'll be powerful upset if you harm either of them." He smiled the entire time he was telling them to get the hell out of his town; it was sort of disconcerting to Lee. "Them is nice young women, and one of them is my granddaughter-in-law. You don't want to mess with her family. They'll kill you where you stand."

He just walked away after telling them he hoped they had a nice meal. Hazel was looking at him like he felt right now — a bit shocked, of course, but also a little afraid, he didn't mind thinking. What the hell did they tell these people, anyway, to have them treating them like this? Lee asked Hazel what she thought about it all.

"I don't care what they're saying about us so long as we can get Carter where we want her. Tomorrow after we have breakfast here, we'll ask Rachel to have a nice meal with us, to get caught up on things. We'll take her back to our hotel, have her call Carter and tell her that we have her, and be done with this place." He asked her if she thought that was going to work. "Yes, I do. They both are going to have to learn that we're their bosses, and what we say goes. And we are running out of time here. Those men are going to be here tomorrow night to take their delivery and pay us. We have to move this along now."

He told her that he knew that but was worried that everyone seemed to know what they were doing here. And it wasn't like they'd been quiet, either, when talking to Rachel. Hazel told him not to worry about it. This town was small, and small towns were always in other people's business. And if they thought to get in their way, they'd take them out if they tried anything with them.

"We're in the right here, Lee, you know that. Once we have our money, they'll never hear from us again." He said that was true. "And I don't know about you, but I'm looking forward to settling down in my own home with my own things, and not worrying about anything but us."

For some reason he didn't think it was going to be that easy. Sure, they could tell Rachel to go with them to the hotel and have her call Carter, but he was reasonably sure that she'd not do it easily. And Carter was going to be hostile toward them too. It bore thinking about a secondary plan. Just in case this one fell apart, like he thought perhaps it would.

Chapter 9

Carter sat at the booth and tried to enjoy her breakfast with Josh. They'd been there for the last thirty minutes just waiting for her parents. She was sort of sick to her stomach right now, and was sure she was going to have to go and throw up again. Instead of letting it get to her again, she sipped her tea.

Tea. She was drinking tea now. Not that it wasn't good, because it was, but she hated having someone make a pot for her when she went to their house. Most of the time she just drank water so they'd not, but she wanted something to settle her belly, and the tea had done it at home before they left.

Dylan was waiting tables with Rachel. She wasn't as good at it as her sister was, but people liked her so that worked out well. Ollie was running the register and having a good time. The man could talk your arm off if he had a captive audience. He was also having a couple of biscuits while he worked. This was after he'd eaten a huge breakfast before the place opened.

She laughed when he turned and winked at her—the man was about the cutest and sweetest man she had ever met. Besides Josh, that was. When he started talking about the weather, she wondered how many ways a person could say it was blustery out without repeating themselves. Ollie was doing a fine job of it so far.

Carter knew that her parents were in town. That they were parking their car around back of the restaurant. Their plan was to get Rachel outside, then knock her out. If she screamed or did anything that would draw attention to them, they'd simply kill her. Carter could not believe that they were so cold.

"Blake said that they just parked by the dumpster around back. You know that, correct?" Carter nodded at Josh, and he took her hand into his. "This is going to work, love. It was just our good fortune that Dylan was able to track down the guy that is going to buy you from them. And with the email that she sent him, he'll be showing up here too."

"Yes, I know. And Adrian is going to tell them that the gig is up, and that the police and agents are here to talk to them. I know that's what we hope will happen, but I know that you understand that anything could and will go wrong." He squeezed her hand and she saw them come in the door. "They're here. And good Christ, they sure have gotten old."

Josh burst out laughing, which brought her parents' attention to them. They looked at them both, but didn't seem to recognize Carter. That's what Dylan was hoping for. After ten years without seeing her, they'd be surprised by her being there with Rachel. When they were seated in Rachel's section, all was going according to plan. But Carter was going to be ready, just in the event that things started to not go the way that they wanted them to go.

When their order was taken, Rachel moved away

from them. She could feel their disappointment at her not cooperating, and they were going to have to work a bit harder, Carter thought. Just as they were being served their breakfast, a stranger came into the diner and sat alone in one of the booths. He was talking to Ollie when her father grabbed Rachel's arm.

"Now see here, I just want to have a nice long talk with you." Everyone in the diner turned to look at her father while he spoke in hissed tones to Rachel. "Come now, we've not seen you in years, the least you can do is have a meal with us."

"I told you no. Now, I'd like for you to unhand me before I knock the shit out of you. I'm not a kid anymore, and I won't put up with your shit."

Rachel jerked from their dad and moved away. While she waited on other customers, she was as polite as she'd ever been.

"It's time."

She stood up after telling Josh she had this. Moving toward her parents, she saw the stranger do the same. Reaching into his mind, she paused and waited for him to reach her parents and sit down. Carter moved to sit with Josh's grandda who'd returned to the counter.

He's the man that they're selling me to. He's pissed off that they're making such a scene in here, when all he wants to do is gather his goods — I'm guessing he means me — and then go. Josh asked her what his plan was. *Josh, tell your family not to move.*

The man stood up then, his gun out where everyone could see it. "Everyone, this is just a friendly exchange of goods here, and I don't want any trouble." He turned then and shot both her mother and father in the head before continuing. "Change

133

of plans. Rachel, you're to come with me."

"It's me you want." She couldn't let her sister be taken. Not only would she not survive with him any more than she would have her parents, but Carter thought she was better able to handle the man. "I'm Carter. The person you want to take with you."

"Well, aren't you just helpful." He shot Rachel then, and when she fell back, Josh caught her. "Now, you're going to come with me, all quiet like, and no one is going to try and stop us."

Is she okay? Josh said that she was going to be all right. *Don't do anything stupid. Have Dylan go out to the air strip. He has a plane there that he's going to try and take me away in. There are four men inside waiting for him.*

I don't want you to go. Please, just take care of him here. She said that there were just too many people. *Then I'm going with you. Carter, you're my mate. I can't let anything happen to you.*

Nothing will. I promise you, I will be just fine. But he'll figure out too late that I'm not one to fuck with. He laughed a little. *What? You don't think I can do that?*

"Are you fucking listening to me?" She looked at the man when he grabbed her arm. "I said, let's go. I don't have all fucking day."

"No, you really don't. But I'm ready."

She walked in front of him as he back stepped to the door. The gun was pointed at her head, but for reasons that she couldn't explain, Carter wasn't worried about that. None of the people in the diner moved, and for that she was glad. As soon as they were outside, three other men grabbed her and shoved her in the back of the van that was running and waiting on them.

"You have no tears for your poor dead parents? They should have known that this deal was going to go sour on them. Stupid people." As someone else drove she was cuffed in chains and a gag was put over her mouth. Since she wasn't required to answer anything, she reached beyond the van to talk directly to Dylan.

You scared the fucking shit out of me. What the hell do you think you're doing, just going with them like it's a trip in the fucking zoo? Josh is frantic — your parents are both dead. Sorry, no loss there, I'm guessing. And your sister is shot. She asked her if she was going to be all right. *Yes, Josh called in some extra help, and she's going to be fine. She might glow in a couple of weeks, but — I'm not done being pissed off at you.*

The people in the diner were going to be killed if I didn't do something. Dylan told her that was a good call then. *Thank you so much. Will she really glow? Never mind. There are four in the van with me, not including the guy with the gun. I'm currently chained up, but I'm not worried about that.*

I'm at the airport now with the troops. There were enough of them there before to take them down should it get nasty, but you said that this was going to make it so that no one is killed, right? She told her just the bad guys. *Yes, all right, I can live with that. And until you say so, I'm to wait on you. Are you sure this is going to work?*

Positive. Once we're at the strip, then I'll take care of them all. Dylan was still skeptical about the way she wanted to do this. *I promise you that no one will be hurt if they do just what you told them. Just let me do my thing and I'll be all right as well.*

I don't want you hurt either. I've grown kinda attached to you and your weirdness. Just stay all right and I won't have to shoot you myself. Carter laughed and felt better for it. *All right, we're in position. And his pilot isn't who he brought. Good idea that, I'll have to remember that in the future.*

My pleasure. But I'm sure you would have thought of it sooner or later. Dylan told her that she would have just popped him in the back of the head and been done with it. *Then what would you have done if the bad guys were all pilots too?*

They wouldn't have gotten that far, trust me. All right, I see a blue van coming up the road. That you? She said it was. *All right. Just remember, we're here if you need us, and be sure not to get dead. Josh would never forgive me.*

Me either.

She felt the van stop and the man, she knew his name now, was pointing the gun at her again. After telling Dylan all their names, she got out when he told her to. Things were going just as she had thought they would. And when Reed Hunt put the gun to her head while they unchained her, she looked around the strip.

There wasn't anyone just walking about, not like there had been when they were out here just the other day. There were cars in the lot, but they belonged to the men working for Dylan. All the people inside were working for her as well. If possible, she was told, don't kill Hunt.

My boss wants to question him. Go figure. I think he wants to know who he works for. Carter told her. *Ah, forgot about that freaky thing you could do. All right, good to know. We're all set up in here. Just bring them in and do your thing.*

Carter was going to wait until they were out on the landing strip before she took care of them all. That way the building wouldn't be hurt, nor would any of the men that were with Dylan. And from the looks of it, she had a fucking army with her. When she was taken to the plane, she closed her eyes and let out a long slow breath. It was time.

~~~

Dylan spoke to Josh four times in ten minutes, each time telling him that Carter was just fine, that her men were as well, and the bad guys were all taken care of. She wasn't sure what to tell him about how they were taken care of, but she knew that justice was served.

Hunt was sitting on the ground, his pants wet from where he'd pissed himself, and babbling about thunderstorms and the hand of God. She was sort of freaked out too, but she was handling it much better than he was. She went to talk to Carter now that things were calmed down.

"Remind me never to piss you off." Carter was looking a little shell shocked herself. "You okay? I've told Josh you are. He's nearly here, by the way."

"Yes, I'm all right. A little lightheaded, but I guess that's to be expected. Did anyone else get hurt?" She told her no one that didn't need it. "Two of your men, they were in on it, did you know that?"

"Not until they fell to the floor screaming. Did you know before coming here?" She said not until she came into the building. "Thanks for that then. They'll be taken care of as well. Hunt pissed himself. Funniest thing I ever saw, I have to tell you. And when all those men.... What the hell did you do to them, anyway? Or do I want to know."

"I took care of them." Dylan wasn't satisfied, and Carter seemed to know it. "They're dead, as you know. But I raped each of their minds to get you all the information that you needed. By the way, the two men that were in on it, they have families that are just as guilty. I hope you don't mind, but they're being detained at the airport in Columbus."

"One of my men there notified me that they were there. He said that they just walked right up to him and told him what they were doing. I don't suppose you had anything to do with that, did you?" Carter just shrugged at her. "Carter, can we talk about what happened here today?"

"Yes. I killed them." Dylan was sure that it was more than that, but wasn't sure how to ask her. "I got information from them. Then I killed them."

"Yes, you did. But how did you do it? I won't have to explain how they were killed to anyone but my boss, but I'd like to know. Are you that dangerous to have as an enemy?"

"Only to those that mean to hurt anyone in my family." She looked up at her then. "I'd never harm you or any of the others. But I will protect you in ways that you cannot imagine. I found out their choice of how they like to torture people, and I used the same on them. And they all had killed—most of them would have continued on this path until they were stopped. I was just in the right place at the right time to do so."

"One of them was standing close to me. I saw his body start to slice open along his face and arms. It took me a moment to figure out that he was doing it to himself. I was so shocked by what he was doing. Then he started on his legs. They were being sliced open as well, and if the amount of blood was any indication, he cut an artery." Carter only nodded. "Then he opened his throat and fell to his knees. Like he was some kind of fucking magical show and he was the main attraction."

"He'd done worse to others. One of the men that was standing next to me pissed on the floor, and then took the electrical cover off and electrocuted himself. I had no idea what he'd done until then. When I searched their minds, I saw that they were sadistic fucks. But when I put out that they were to perish by their own hands, I didn't know how they'd die." Carter stood up. "Will it be too hard for you to explain?"

"No. I'll just tell him what you told me. They died by their own hands. That'll be all he needs to know."

Dylan looked over at the two men that had died in the most horrific way she'd ever seen. At first it was just their pecs they'd cut off, then their dicks, laughing and seemingly having a good time while they were at it. She had a feeling that those two would be going straight to hell, and no getting two hundred bucks for passing go either.

"Carter?" She turned back to her and looked so serene, like she had not just killed eighteen men without touching them. "I'm not going to put in my report what really happened here. And I've spoken to a buddy of mine, Tanner the vampire, that helped your sister. He's taken care that my men only know that they're dead. If this were to get out, there would be no place you could hide."

"I know that. And I thank you. Do you think that anyone in the family wishes that I'd never come to them?" She asked her why she'd think that. "For the same reason that you're not going to say anything to anyone. I'm a monster."

"You're not anything of the kind. I've seen these men and the way that they killed themselves. Those are the monsters. And you helped so that they're no longer a threat to anyone." Carter still didn't look convinced. "What can I do so you'll know that without your help today, this would have gone to shit?"

"Nothing. I don't think. I'll have to come to my own terms, I guess." She started away. Dylan could see the family car coming down the road. When she stopped and turned

139

toward her, Dylan could see the tears that filled her eyes, and she herself got a little emotional as well. "Waldo will be a piece of cake after this."

Dylan had work to do, but she did worry about Carter. She was close to the edge, anyone could see that. And when Josh held her, she thought that might be just what the doctor ordered. Turning to one of her men, she asked him where they were in all this.

"We've taken apart the plane, like you said. Sir, you're not going to believe what we found in it. This guy was set for some kind of war, I'm thinking. And the cage that he has in the cargo area, it was ready to be airdropped some place, we're thinking."

She followed him to the plane that she'd put guards around the moment things were finished here. There were grenades and short-range missiles. Guns of every make and model that she'd ever used. And there was enough ammo to do just what the soldier had told her—finish up a nice sized war. In the cargo area was the cage. In addition to that, there were more guns, a Jeep—Army issued, she'd bet anything— as well as more guns still in crates. She pulled out her phone and made a call.

"Henry, we have a problem here." He laughed and asked her if she ever did a mission where there wasn't a problem. When she didn't laugh with him, he abruptly turned serious. "What is it? More men coming?"

"No, but I'm standing in the belly of their plane, and there are Army issued weapons here. Not to mention uniforms, as well as a few dozen long range devices. A dozen or so drones, as well as any and every gun you'd need to have a nice standoff if necessary." He asked her where the plane was now. "Sitting in a tiny airport in Zanesville. I have a feeling that this was just picked up or was going someplace for cash. I'm thinking the first option. Don't know why, but that's my gut feeling."

"Your gut hasn't been wrong before. I'm sending you some...no, that won't work. We don't know who is in on this. I don't suppose you have a way of finding out, do you?" She said that she could ask, but he was going to owe her. "I can handle that. I imagine that she's sitting pretty high about now. Everyone out to get her is gone."

"Actually, she's depressed. Go figure. And afraid that my new family is going to turn her out to the pasture. Much like you guys did when I was hurt." He laughed, but he was nervous. "Let me get back to you. But I'm serious. She's in a bad way, and anything you could do for her would help."

"I'll see what I can do for her. In the meantime, you get what you can from her and I'll look into this from my end. Who knows but you?" She told him just one man. Then she explained how two of the men Henry had sent out here were in on this thing. "Do you think they were put there to help with the load rather than the girl? If so, that'll narrow down considerably who did this. The man who recruited them for you."

She told him to hang on a moment and she'd ask. Henry knew that Carter had been helpful in all this, but not in what capacity. And Dylan decided to keep it that way. Not that she didn't trust Henry, she did. But this was something that could get a great many people hurt. Reaching out to Carter, she asked her what she knew about the shipment.

I'd have to see it. I mean, it's not like people, I can't read them. But like Sunny, I can touch it and tell where it's been for you. She asked her if they could do that. *I can, but Josh said that he's not leaving me. He'll have to come as well.*

That's fine. I don't know who to trust that's here. She didn't say anything for several minutes, and that scared her more than her telling her what she'd done to the men that were dead. *Carter? Everything all right?*

Yes. You can trust all the men that are here with you. And for the record, none of them know what was in the plane other than the cage that was put in a couple of days before they left Washington. I'm nearly there.

Dylan told Henry that she'd call him back after telling him that the plane left from Washington. "As soon as I know, you'll know."

She was waiting for Carter and Josh when they came up the stairs. Josh looked better than he had when she'd seen him earlier today. She wondered if he knew that his shirt was covered in blood, but didn't think he'd care. The man had been so tense for so long that she found that she really liked this new version of her brother-in-law. He was laid back yet on the ready all the time.

Carter walked around the belly of the plane. She didn't touch anything, and it wasn't until Josh told her what she was doing that she knew why. She was looking for any kind of sign that the weapons had been touched by a person and not a crane. Dylan thought that made sense, but she did want her to hurry.

"Dylan, what do you know of a man by the name of Winston Gill?" She told her that he was one of the recruiters for the special forces, and he was someone that worked tightly with the president and her when she was there. Carter nodded. "Is he the one that ordered this shit?"

"He's one of them. There are two more that are aware of this shipment. This was to be taken to an airstrip in Nevada and picked up there to move to Mexico. The trucks are waiting there to unload and transport." Dylan asked who the other two men were. "Not men, but women. One of them is Gill's wife. Megan is a booking agent for a very small travel agency. It's a front for moving arms. The other woman is her secretary, May Winthrop. This is the fifth shipment that has gone out."

"Christ." She called Henry again and told him what she'd found out. "This is the fifth one, Henry. They've been moving arms right under our fucking noses. This is treason, not to mention it's pissed me off. Mother fuck, this is bad. Now what do we do?"

"I'll have them arrested before this hits the news. In a sweep, so as not to warn the other two so that they don't take off." He cursed then too, and she had to smile. He was usually so reserved about this sort of thing, but he was pissed off now. "You take care there so that I can know that it's not going to start up again. However you want to do it."

"I can do that. My plan now is to take the plane to Nevada and make a few arrests there. Once I have that under control, then I'll bring everything back to you." She saw that Carter was trying to get her attention. "Hang on. I need a minute."

"The men in Nevada aren't in on it. They're only hired to do transporting. They think that they're moving bottled water to a warehouse." Well, that explained why everything was in large crates. She asked her if there was anyone there that knew. "Yes, Winthrop. She's coordinating everything there. And picking up the cash."

After telling Henry what was going on, she got her pilot

and made sure that everything on the plane was the way it was. Josh and Carter got off, but before she did, Carter told her what Winthrop was wearing and what she looked like. Dylan didn't know why that was important, but was glad for all the help she could get. It was time to have herself a bit of fun.

Chapter 10

Josh went straight to their house from the airport. He needed his mate right now, more than he ever had before. As soon as they were in the door, he didn't just take her clothing off but tore it from her body. She did the same to him as they hungrily kissed each other.

When she was as naked as he was, he picked her up and slammed his cock into her heat. There was no need for foreplay this time; their need for each other more than made up for playing around until they were ready.

She came twice before he could sample her breasts. Josh was on edge; his cat was tearing at his skin to keep her safe. Up until this moment he'd been quiet, but now he was angry at their mate and wanted her to understand that she'd scared them both. Biting her on the shoulder drew a scream of pain from her, but pleasure too. The next time she came, he pounded her harder until he was able to release in her as well.

Leaning against her, he finally was able to lift his head from her shoulder. When she asked him to take her to bed, he was more than willing to do that. He now needed to make it up to her, make love to her slowly and thoroughly. Still holding her, he kissed her on the mouth and started for the stairs.

"You should know that you're not leaving the bed until I'm satisfied that you're safe and here." She hugged him. "We were all right until we saw the bodies. I think that my cat thought he'd find you, and no matter how many times I told him you were safe, he needed to see you."

They were in their room by now, and he set her on the floor while he kissed her tenderly. He noticed that she was bruised in a couple of places where he'd hurt her, and kissed those areas as well. Carter started talking as he was making his way to her pretty ass.

"I'm not sure what to think about today." He asked her not to talk about it. "All right, but you have to distract me. I'm having a hard time dealing right now."

He got down on his knees in front of her and kissed her right above the small line of hair over her pussy. Sliding his fingers into her, he asked her what she was thinking about now. At her grin, he knew that it was working.

"I'm thinking about the way you took me like an animal downstairs, and how much I enjoyed that." Josh licked her from gate to clit, then nibbled on the hard nubbin peeking from her nether lips. "I was thinking about—don't stop, please—I was thinking about a baby. We should have one, or a dozen."

"I'd love that. What do you want first?" He was teasing her now, having entirely too much fun when a moan spilled from her mouth as an answer. "I want them to be healthy as well. That's a priority."

"What if they're like me?" He said that it didn't matter to him. "But I killed people today."

He stood up and pulled her face to his. The kiss was consuming, powerful, and heated. When he looked down at her, he could see the tears and held her to him. Josh wanted to hide her away so that no one could hurt her ever again.

"You did. And you saved a great many other people too. Dylan for one. Her men as well. I know that you lost your parents, and I'm sorry for that, but you're here, with me and safe." She nodded. "Also, I think you should know that my entire family is so glad that this part is over, and is going to welcome you with lots of hugs. Grandda is acting like he taught you everything you know."

"I love that old man. He's such a hoot. And he told me that he was going to be my grandda as well. That I could call him that whenever I wanted. I've never had a one before that I can remember."

He picked her up again and took her to the bed. This time he only held her, rubbing her arms so that he could touch her. When she turned to him, sobbing about today, he let her, knowing that sometimes tears were what it took to cleanse the soul.

After about twenty minutes, he knew that she'd fallen asleep. Josh knew that she'd not slept well for the past two nights, worrying about all this crap with her parents and what they might do. So when he knew that she'd not wake up, he slipped out from under her head and covered her up with the blanket at the bottom of the bed. Getting dressed, he kept an eye on her to see if she was resting all right. She seemed to be out for a while.

Going downstairs, he made his way to his office after

picking up the things in the front hall that they'd torn up. He was glad now that the staff was off for the morning and they'd not come upon them when they were naked. Smiling, he went to the kitchen to get him something to snack on while he worked for a little while.

There were several houses on the market right now. And even though he wasn't working, he was always looking for a good buy to make his portfolio stronger. One thing his grandma used to say all the time was, there wasn't going to be any more dirt, so you should take care that you own as much of it as you can. He had never forgotten that.

Josh had been looking at the houses when he came across one that he really liked. Not that he was going to buy it, but he did call his brother Adrian and told him about it. It was perfect for him when his mate showed up, Josh told him.

"Very funny. And thank you, but no thanks. On the mate anyway. But tell me about the house. The one that came with the job, I'm not thrilled about it. It looks to me like it was decorated in the seventies and never updated. I mean, the appliances are fine, but it's the décor that I hate." He pointed out that he could change that. "No. I'm not going to be spending tax payers' money on new wallpaper, even if this orange and green shit makes me ill every time I move my head."

"I'm sending you the link to your email." When he said he had it, they both went over the pictures. "There is sixty plus acres that come in the price, but there is an additional fifty that can be purchased for a song that butts up against Mom and Dad's place." He noticed that Waldo had some land there too, and tried to remember who had told him that. "There's a long drive to the house that has a guard shack out front.

You'll need to be using that soon, if I were you. You being a big shot, that could be unsafe for you."

"I love that it has an inground pool too."

They talked about all the things that were in the house, as well as some of the improvements that would need to be made. Security from Dylan's men would have to be done as well.

"Can you get me a better price?" He said that he probably could; the house had been sitting on the market for three months. "Have you really decided to quit your job? I mean, you seemed to have loved it when you did it."

"I did, but now I feel as if I've got better things to do with my time. Carter is not demanding my time, but I do love spending time with her and just sitting around the house. I'm sure that I'll be bored soon enough, but for now, I'm happy." Adrian told him he could come by his place anytime he wanted. "I'll do that. If you hang on a second, I can make them an offer right now. They have it set up on the page to do that."

Josh noticed that the house had been on the market for three months with the realtor that they had now, but over a year before that with someone else. He thought that was a long time to be selling a house, and the price had been reduced several times already. Putting in what he thought was a reasonable price for the house, he told Adrian what he'd done.

"I went by Evan's home this morning. That garden out back is a showplace. I've never seen so many flowers and vinery things in my life. Flora is doing a fantastic job, and she loves the place too." Josh said that she was going to help him with the herb garden in the back of his house, as well as help him pick out things to put around the house for the faeries. "I might have her do that for me if I get the house."

His email dinged that he had a new message and he laughed, telling Adrian that he had the house. He asked if they had wanted a counter offer or anything. Josh told him that they were more than likely glad to have it off their hands.

"Now all you have to do is sign the paperwork and move in. Well, it'll be a little more than that, but you have a home you can be proud of." He knew the house; he'd shown it a couple of times recently. But the house was mammoth, and people didn't want houses that big anymore. The one that Blake had bought was almost as large.

After telling him that he'd get the paperwork to him in a couple of days, he closed up his computer and went out on the deck. It was still pretty out, but would be cold soon. He was going to be an uncle too, he just remembered. Sunny was big with hers and David's baby, and he couldn't have been more happy for them both.

When arms wrapped around him from behind, he held Carter to him by holding her hand. When she came to stand in front of him, he kissed her and asked her how she'd slept.

"Pretty good, as a matter of fact. What have you been doing?" He told her about the house and what his brother was going to be doing. "I'm happy for him. Having a house is a lot nicer than I thought it would be."

"What would you like to do now?" She looked away, then back at him, and he felt his heart clench up. "Honey, don't cry. Whatever it is, we can handle it."

"The funeral home called. They want me to come and make arrangements for my parents. I talked to Rachel, and she said that they could rot in a hole for all she cared. I feel the same way. I'm just sad that this turned out the way that it did. So many people died today." He said it was what they deserved. "I knew you were going to say that."

"Have you an idea what you want to do with them? And I'll have someone looking into their records at their home. Perhaps there is a will or something there that can be used." She told him what she wanted to do. "That's probably for the best. Having them cremated, then a small family service later is what I'd do too."

"It's not like they knew anyone around here. And I'm sure that no one would care that they're dead where they lived either. They had some things at the hotel that I'm having shipped here—I hope you don't mind. The hotel was very polite about it when I called and asked. I thought we could just use something they had in their bags to take care of them in." He nodded and said that was good too. "Rachel wants me to come by and see her. I guess they're keeping her overnight just to be sure. She said that she feels great, but she did bump her head."

"Tanner gave her a little of his blood, so she'll be fine in a couple of days if not sooner. All the people at the diner are concerned that she won't be coming back to work. Shirley said that she's the best thing that's happened to her little place since she bought the new mixer for the mashed potatoes."

"Well, that's high praise if you ask me. Her mashed potatoes are to die for." They were both laughing when George came in to ask if they wanted to have a light snack before dinner was started. "Yes. I would love something. Do you have any more of those scones that you served me yesterday morning? They were blackberry, I think."

"They were berries of all sorts, ma'am. I think there are

151

one or two of them left. Coffee or tea, mistress?" She told him tea, and then he asked Josh what he wanted. When he was gone, she sat on the couch with Josh.

"I could really get used to this, I think." He told her that he was already loving it. "Me too. Just one more jackass to take care of, and we're going to be just fine."

He was still laughing about that when their scones and tea were brought to them. There were three of them left, and she managed to eat two before Josh finished his one. Suddenly, she was starving.

~~~

Carter read over the email three times that had come to her. And each time she read it, she was no less dumbfounded by what it said. When Josh joined her in the little room she'd taken as her own, she had him read it over.

"It's from Henry. I did tell you that he was a good friend of the family's, didn't I?" She said that he had, but this was her personal email. "I'm sure that he has ways about him to get your email address, honey."

Okay, there was that. Him being the leader of the country, he'd have access to all sorts of things. But he had congratulated her on her upcoming wedding, and told her how helpful she'd been in the capture of arms being sold to other countries. And that he was sending her a gift that he hoped she'd cherish as much as he did her.

"How did he get the info...Dylan. Okay, that explains a great deal. But I wasn't all that helpful in the capture of those men. Dylan was the one that went there and gathered up the mastermind. You know, I had no idea that she was the one moving things around to suit herself."

Winthrop had not just been the mastermind of the entire

thing, but she had several off-shore accounts, money all over her home, and cash out the ass in her office drawers. It all amounted to several billion dollars.

"Dylan said this would go down as Henry's greatest victory, and no one would know that you and she played any role in it whatsoever." Carter told him she was fine with that. "Yeah, Dylan said that same thing. She's like you in that, a behind the scenes sort of person. But I'm to understand that she'll get a promotion, as well as a bonus."

"That's good for her. It was a pleasure working with her." She looked at Josh when he sat down on the little love seat that was in her office. "She didn't try and take over, ever. When we had to change plans, I was sure that she was going to tell me that she'd take over. But the first thing out of her mouth was what did I want to do. I felt like I was really part of something huge."

"You were. And the people that know you were are very proud of you." She felt her face warm in embarrassment. "Speaking of people proud of you, our wedding is in the morning. Are you ready to become Mrs. Joshua Whitfield for real?"

"I am. More than you can guess. However, I've been called that so much lately, it's almost like we are married already." She went to him and sat on his lap. As far as she was concerned, it was the best place to be. "Josh, do you think you could teach me to drive?"

"Really? You don't know how to drive?" She told him that was on her list of things to do when she ended up in prison. "Oh. Yes, I'd love to teach you to drive. However, I can't. I want us to stay happy, and teaching someone you love how to drive is a good way to argue. And you can't learn from Dylan either. For as bad assed as she is, she drives ten times worse. Taking a curve with her driving is like riding on roller blades."

"Then who do you suggest? Your mom is afraid to teach me. She said that she doesn't drive all that much anymore, and has more than likely forgotten more than she ever learned about it. Your dad is just too busy." He asked her about Grandda. "You think he'd do it? That would be fantastic. And I love that old man."

"Yes, well, he loves you as well. And I think he'd be really good at it. He's not one of those older men who drive like they're afraid to use the gas pedal, and he's been driving for as long as I think there have been cars." She laughed with him, and thought of learning to drive from Ollie. "You should ask him at dinner. I'm sure that he'll love to do it."

She sat there thinking of all the things that had happened in the last few days. Rachel was doing so much better that she had already returned to work. Rachel loved waiting tables, it seemed, and she was really good at it. And Shirley just loved her.

She'd taken care that her parents were cremated. Rachel didn't want anything to do with their service, or anything else that happened to them. Carter was just fine with that and told her that she'd take care of it. There wasn't anything put in the local paper; no one would have known them, and she only put a small obit in the paper where they had lived.

Reed Hunt had been taken to military prison, along with the others that were involved with the selling of arms. Even though he'd not been a part of the ring, because he'd been in the plane that was carrying the weapons meant for selling, his name was put on the list of people who had committed treason as well. That way no one but them would know that he'd been a part of something that had to do with her.

"We're going take care of Waldo tonight. It's the night of his big deal, I guess. And from what I've heard, his clients aren't very happy about their accommodations. They're all the way in Columbus, which is a good hour from here. And there isn't that homey feeling that he promised them." She said good, it served him right. "We are also having a little trouble finding out who he took from the shelter. There are six men missing, but we don't think he could have handled that many at once."

"You guys don't think he's gotten himself help?" Josh told her that they'd been watching him coming and going for two weeks now, and it appeared to be just him. "Did you find out anything about Tommy? You said that he just disappeared."

"He's dead. One night about a week after you came here, Tommy came upon Tanner when he was feeding. Tanner said that he'd been very careful, shadows pulled around them so that no one would know. But as soon as he was finished putting money in the man's pocket, Tanner came at him with a ball bat." Carter asked if Tanner had been hurt. "No, not really he told me. But he couldn't get the man to back off—it was like he was crazy possessed or something. He ended up killing him by tearing his throat out. Then he took him home to the address on his driver's licenses. Tanner had no idea that it was the same man that we'd been having trouble with."

"It's probably just as well, I guess. One less person that we have to concern ourselves with over this thing." Josh told her that's what the rest of them had said too. "I'm looking forward to going on our honeymoon. Going away for real, not holed up in our house waiting for a madman to come along and try to kill another human being."

"I have been thinking the same thing. After this is done, as you said, we're going to spend about a month touring Ireland and all the other regions around there. Tanner said that we could use his homes while there, and he'd pay us to see if things are in working order." Carter asked him if he'd turned him down on the money. "I did, but you know how he can be. Anyway, he's made us reservations at restaurants while we're visiting his homes. All paid for. I think that'll be fun too."

She just wanted things to be normal. However, for as much time as she'd spent in prison, she had no clue what normal would entail. Carter asked Josh if they thought this thing with Waldo would go as smoothly as they were hoping it would.

"The police have it under control here. And we have a lot of extra people here too that are going to be watching out for the townspeople. I don't know that it will go without a hitch, but there shouldn't be any major issues. Waldo comes onto our land and we have him arrested, along with the men that paid him to kill a person. That's premeditated, and that is going to get their sorry asses in a lot of shit." She knew that as well. But she wasn't to help them in any way.

"Dylan said that these men will go to jail, and that if they see me doing anything odd or out of the ordinary, they'll tell someone who could make it so that we'll have to look over our shoulders for a long time." He said that's what she'd told him as well. "I hate not being able to make sure that they're all right."

"I know you do, honey, but this is for the best. I don't want to have you hurt any more than I do Dylan and the rest of them. But you have to see that she's right on this. We're just lucky that the men who came to get you in the first place are all taken care of. That way, no one knows what happened here but you and a few others."

They were right, but it didn't make her feel any better about any of this. They were to sit tight and let anyone know when they saw strangers on their land. The pack was out wandering around too, and knew to be extra careful. Idiots with guns were no one they needed to be around.

At about four-thirty, they were told that a car had pulled onto the property that Waldo had purchased. When six men got out, they'd been a little worried. They were only counting on five, including Waldo. But one of them was the driver, and Dylan told them that it wouldn't be long now. They saw the first man darting by their house not ten minutes later.

Evan and the other brothers were out roaming the property too. They were going to get the men who had been captured as prey and take them into the shelter that they'd put up for them. The first man, they'd heard, had been found, and they were looking for the next prey, as they were calling them. The men walked by their home with their rifles over their shoulders like this was a big game hunting trip. She was so mad that she wanted to go out there and shoot them a few times and see how they liked it. Josh called the police and told them that there were four men on his land with guns.

Josh went out on the deck just as Waldo came running back from the wooded part of their house. He'd been bitten, it looked like to her, and he was being chased by a group of the pack. She was laughing so hard at him running and holding up his pants that she had to sit down. The police were at his home waiting for him. And after that, Tanner would

KATHI S. BARTON

take care that he died either in the jail or soon after. It was sort of anticlimactic after all the preparation that they'd gone through to make this happen. And when they gathered up the other men, all treed by wolves and tigers, it seemed, they found that not only did they have the sitting governor of their state, but also a few more that should know better.

She wondered if any of them remembered that they had a gun while up in the tree waiting for someone to rescue them. Carter told Josh that if these men were to take care of the state, she was more worried now than before about how things were going. They were laughing as the police came by and told them that they'd caught them all.

Joshua

Chapter 11

Adam didn't even know that anything was going on around Josh's house. He'd been so buried in his work that he'd barely had enough time to take a shower, much less keep up on the news. When he put the tractor away for the last time this year, he felt a sense of accomplishment that he did every year at this time.

The hay was all bailed and sitting in the barn. There were rolls of alfalfa, too, that they would give to whoever needed it during the winter. It was something that his family had been doing for years to help out their neighbors. The garden that he put in every year was all finished, and all he had left to harvest was the pumpkins that he loved growing.

Adam grew an entire field of the small pumpkins for the kids to come out and pick at no cost. The buses would start coming around in about a week, and he'd have kids all over the place. He thought that was why Halloween was his favorite time of the year. The kids made all his hard work so worth it.

He saw Blake coming in from the other field about the time he was getting off the tractor. They were going to hang out at Adam's house tonight like old times.

"I heard that that guy, whatever his name was—all I can think of is a striped red shirt—was caught." Adam laughed with his brother, then he told him his name. "Yeah, that's it. Anyway, I just heard from Mom that they're all finished up and that they're going to Josh and Carter's house for some dinner. We were invited too, but I told them you and I had plans."

"Good. I've been looking forward to this all day. And the thought of just taking off my boots and sitting down with my feet propped up, I can't tell you how excited I am about that."

Blake agreed and said he'd be back in an hour. He had to shower and change. Adam told him that he'd order their dinner.

After getting his own shower, he ordered six large heavy meat pizzas. They'd probably only eat four or five of them, but he wanted cold pizza for his breakfast tomorrow. He knew it was odd, but he really liked cold pizza to start his day off.

When Blake retuned, they still had ten or so minutes left before the pizza arrived. Adam pulled out his computer and showed Blake his crop reports, and his plan for the following planting season. Blake was impressed, and said he might steal a couple of his ideas.

As soon as they paid the guy for their dinner, giving him a hefty tip because he'd kept them hot for them, they sat down at the dining room table and ate three of them before they even spoke a word other than just grunting.

"You thinking about your mate?" Adam asked why he'd be thinking about that. "Don't know, really, but when I'm driving through the fields, I gotta have something to occupy my mind. It's boring as fuck just going back and forth through the field like that."

"Yeah, you're right. I've taken to listening to books while I'm driving. It's sort of like having television, but no pictures. And they're usually not too bad. You should try it." Blake said that he would. "But what about a mate? Have you some clue that yours is coming?"

"Naw. I was just thinking of the other three and how they're all cozied up with a woman all the time. It would be nice, I think, to have someone around that you could talk to all the time. I just hope that she's more stimulating than driving the tractor for hours on end." Adam said he surely hoped so as well. "I've been going over my plans with the house and all. I've applied for adoption of one of the kids that was left behind when his family was killed a couple of months back. He's been coming around when he can, and we've hit it off pretty good."

"That's what you bought the big house for, right?" Blake said that it was. "You think your mate will be pissy about having a ready-made family when she comes to you?"

"That's not the way it's supposed to work, is it?" Adam asked him what he meant. "They're supposed to be our other half, right? Well, my other half had better like kids that aren't of her body, because that's what I want to do. Help kids that don't have anyone in their lives but us."

"Why? I mean, it's not like you grew up underprivileged. None of us did. We didn't have everything that we wanted, but enough that we knew that we had money. What makes a man like you want to adopt kids that have no other help?" Blake told him he had family and they didn't. "Yes, all of us would chip in right away if you needed us. I understand you wanting to give them family. But what drives you to want to do this? I think you have a reason. Not that it matters, I guess. You could adopt a couple of dozen kids, and I would think they were the luckiest kids in the world."

"While I'm on this earth I want to make it so that there is one less child go to bed without supper. Hell, I want to give them the bed too. I want to try my best to give a child a place to feel secure and safe. Give them a hug without pain involved. Let them push away from the table because they're full, not because there isn't any more food for them to eat." Adam eyed his brother. These were all wonderful reasons to adopt, yet he thought there was more to it. "Don't look at me like that. I gave you an answer."

"But is it the real answer?" Blake just turned away from him, shutting him out almost. "What happened, Blake? I know you better than the rest of them ever will. What happened that brought this on?"

"They were living in the barn up until a month ago. Three of them. A dad and his two kids. I knew they were there, I could smell them, but they never came out when I was in the barn. So I brought them out some blankets and stuff. Then I started to set food out with a hotplate. I was sort of scared that they'd burn the barn down, but they had to be hungry, right?" Adam nodded. "The little girl came out when I was saddling up the old mare. She needed a good run. The mare, not the little girl. Anyway, she thanked me for the food and blankets. You should have seen her, Adam. She was no bigger than a stick, and she was sallow looking. Like she'd not had a good meal in years. I asked to speak to her daddy, the adult that was with them. And.... Christ, he was dying. Right in the barn. I wanted to take him to the hospital, but he told me it was too late for that. That as soon as his sister came to get the kids, he was moving on. He meant that he was going to let himself die. I started to put out more food, and even some aspirin for the man. They'd not come into the house though, and I think that about tore me apart. Then one day, they were all gone."

"The sister came to get the kids." He said that he didn't know, but that's what he figured. The smell of perfume was there. "Blake, that's the saddest and most wonderful reason I've heard in a long time for doing something good. You need any help with this, you let me know. I'm there for you."

Blake nodded and said that he was heading home. It was nearly midnight when Adam thought that he could go to bed. His brother was going to do something noble with his life, and Adam thought him his greatest hero.

The next morning, he was having breakfast when Sunny came by. She was pacing his kitchen back and forth before she spoke. He'd noticed that about her. She didn't say anything until she had something to say. No emptying out her head just to hear her lips flapping for this one.

"Have you ever babysat before?" He didn't get a chance to answer her before she went on. "I haven't any idea how to change a diaper. I guess I could do it, but I'd fuck it up before I finally got it right. And those sleeper things. Have you had a good look at those suckers? They've got snaps down both legs and then in-between. I think I'd probably piss myself if I had to take something like that off to go to the bathroom."

"They do." She asked him what he meant. "Piss themselves. Thus the need for the diaper. Babies don't use the toilet for years, I guess. And no, I've never babysat."

She sat down across from him then popped up, getting her a bowl and some of his cereal. He watched her move around his kitchen, and wondered what it would be like having a female in the house, doing what Sunny was doing. She sat and ate a bite of the cereal, then shoved it away.

"What the fuck is that? It tastes like rocks and grass." He told her it was whole grain and good for her. "No, that can't be good for you. It's like eating gravel from the driveway. What kind of sick person makes that sort of breakfast food?"

He was laughing when he stood and got her another bowl and spoon. "I have this for when I'm feeling young. And that's not all that often lately. But I have the entire winter to rest up, so I'll have me a bowl of this once in a while."

She poured the sugary treat in the bowl and ate it without milk, popping it into her mouth like it was popcorn. He asked her what she was upset about with the diapers and sleepers. She ate a few more bites before she spoke again.

"I don't want to fuck up on being a mom." Adam laughed. "I'm dead serious. There are so many rules that you have to follow about having a baby. Like, did you know that they have this belly button thing that you have to take care of? The cord. And then if it's a boy and he's been circumcised, then you have to take care of his little wiener too."

"Wiener? Never mind. Okay, I know you might have thought of this, but for some reason came to your bachelor brother-in-law instead. But I'm betting my mom would love to teach you anything you want to know. And she'd know about sleepers and rules. Not that I think you should worry too much about the rules. I'm thinking you're not too terribly stupid, but you did come here for answers, so I can't vouch for that." She smiled at him and his heart broke. It was the saddest smile he'd ever seen. "Don't cry, honey. I was only teasing you."

"I know, but I don't want your mom to worry that I'm going to mess up having her grandchild. She might think that I'm too dumb to raise it on my own, and have someone come and take it from me." He was startled by her reasoning. "She raised you guys to be wonderful men, and I have to compete with that. I'm not nearly as perfect as she is at this stuff."

"I doubt my mom was perfect at the start either. I mean, have you met Evan? He's as fucked up as they come." She laughed, and he felt better for her. "I'll go with you if you want. Or even talk to my mom for you. But I'm thinking that you'll be just fine. And like I said, you're going to be just fine at this mommy stuff."

"Do you really think so?" He told her he was positive that she would be. "Thank you so much. You have no idea how worried I've been. And I didn't want David to know, but I think he's having his doubts about my sanity. I cry a great deal."

"If he has you committed I'll come and see you every day. I promise."

She laughed harder then, and he knew she was going to be just fine. When she left him, he got ready for his work day and went to the barn. Cleaning the equipment was going to take him all day — but then, he'd be ready for spring in a few months.

~~~

Josh was running behind. He had to meet his family at the courthouse in ten minutes, and he was still at home. Telling her what the problem was, she laughed until she had to close the connection and get back to him. He knew that she was telling the rest of them why he was running late.

What do you mean your suit is gone? Son, I'm sure if you looked it would be in your closet. I had it cleaned for you, and that was where George said he was putting it. He went to his closet and looked again. It wasn't in there. Calling down the stairs to George to find it, he went to another bedroom to look in it. *Have you looked in your closet?*

Yes. Several times. It's not in— George came in the room with his suit still wrapped in plastic from the dry cleaners. "Where was it?"

"I am so sorry, sir. I was going to bring it up to your closet, but I got sidetracked when the miss wanted a sandwich. She is such a joy to have around, and I couldn't turn her down." Josh told him that he had the same problem with her. "Yes, well, she and I started talking about this and that, and before I knew it, it was time to start on dinner. I am so terribly sorry."

"That's okay, George. But you have to tell my mom that it wasn't in my closet where I looked." He looked like he might run for cover. "You have to, George. She thinks I'm incompetent. And I give her enough things to make her believe that I am. I don't need a missing suit on top of that."

"I shall tell her today, sir. After the wedding. They are all coming here afterwards still, aren't they?" He told him they were coming as soon as they were pronounced man and wife. "Good. We've been working for several days on things for this special day for the two of you. I don't think I've ever worked for nicer people than the two of you."

"Thank you so much, George, but I have to get dressed to get married."

Every time he said it aloud, he was excited. His beautiful Carter was going to be his wife in about two hours. Then they were all coming back here to celebrate the day with them. He laughed when he thought of the gift that he'd gotten her.

The beautiful bracelet had been in his family for a few generations, and he'd had a pair of earrings made to match it. She had said the other day how she hadn't worn anything girly in forever. He was glad now that he'd let Dylan talk him into doing this.

When he was ready, Josh raced down the stairs, pulling his jacket on with his shoes in his hand. George was at the door with not just a flower for his lapel, but also a cup of tea and some cookies. To tide him over, he told him.

He was fully dressed, with his shoes on his feet, by the time they rolled up in front of the courthouse. Josh nearly ran to get in the building when his mom came out to meet him. George immediately started telling her it was his fault that Josh was late. Kissing her on the cheek, Josh shoved a cookie in his mouth and looked at his mom when she tsked at him.

"I would have thought that you'd have brought out your best manners for today of all days." She fussed with his tie while they were riding up to the third floor in the elevator. "You and your father never could tie a tie right. His is askew right now."

"I'm sure that Grandda is all spit and polished. I think he was as excited, if not more so, than I was about today. It was very special to him to be asked to give her away."

When the doors opened, Evan and Blake were there waiting for him. All his brothers were his best men today, and he couldn't have been happier.

"Two things before we go into the courtroom. Mom bought a few decorations." He asked Evan how many was a few. "More than I think were at our wedding, and we were married in a church. The second thing—Tanner is here, and he said that it's very important that he speaks to you and Carter before you leave today."

"All right. But did he say what it's about?" Blake said he seemed pleased about something. "Oh well, maybe it's about one of his houses or something. No big deal, right?"

Evan shrugged, and he wanted to hit him. Why couldn't he, today of all days, have lied to him? As they made their way into the courtroom, he nearly left again. A few decorations looked to him as if she'd bought out the store. He asked Blake if Carter had seen this yet.

"Not that I'm aware of. And I don't think I'd be the one that told her either. This is so not low key." No, it wasn't. "You think she'll say forget it and go out with me, the better-looking brother?" He growled at Adam when he spoke.

Standing at the front of the room, he thought that it looked pretty. There were flowers all over the room, and ribbons and bows around the tables and gates that led to the main part of the court proceedings. When the music started playing from one of the loud speakers on the wall, Josh looked for Carter. He needed to see her more than he needed the next beat of his heart.

Rachel came through the doorway first. She looked so lovely. Josh thought that Rachel had blossomed in the last few days. There was no more threat of her parents hanging over her, and she seemed genuinely happy to be here in Ohio with Carter. The two of them were closer than he and his brothers, he thought.

The next person through the door was the one that he'd been waiting for. As soon as they stepped fully in the room, she stopped and looked around. Grandda started laughing then, chuckling so hard that he had to hang onto chairs as he brought Carter to him. As soon as he sat down, he stood again and looked at the two of them.

"I want you to know that other than my lovely bride on our wedding day and this beautiful woman here to my right, you are far and away the prettiest little girl that I've seen in a while." He looked at Eve when she smacked him. "Don't go on like that, Eve. I told them other girls the same thing when they were married to one of my grandsons. Didn't I, Sunny? Ain't that right, Dylan? Besides, I didn't go overboard with all these decorations when I heard someone tell you that it's got to be lowkey. This is about as lowkey as you setting off a bomb on Main Street and selling marshmallows and sticks to the affair."

They were laughing again now, and Josh thought that the room was less tense than it had been. When Carter put her hands into his, he knew that he would love her for all time, and that they'd be happy. He was going to make sure that she laughed every day, and that she never went to bed angry with him. That was his vow to her when it was his turn to say it to Carter.

"I promise to love you for all time and beyond. I will make you as happy as you have made me. I will help you raise our children, whether they be of my heart and body or just my heart." She kissed his hand as she continued. "You are my everything. You saved me from being lonely and alone. You, Joshua Whitfield, are my heart and soul."

When they were pronounced man and wife, he kissed her on the mouth, then picked her up and swung her around in his arms. He was married to his best friend, and there wasn't a man in the world that was as happy right now as he was. Of that, he was sure.

The drive home was just the two of them in the limo. He wanted to strip her down right now and mark her, but he knew that if he was late to one more thing today, his mom would have his head. So, they only necked a little—well, a great deal—and tried to stay reasonably neat before going in the house when they arrived.

Nate and his family were there, as well as a great many of the pack. Dylan had made it clear to the pride that they did not have to come to the reception if they didn't want to. It looked to him like most of them were there anyway. He and Carter tried to talk to everyone that they saw. It was a perfect night for this kind of partying.

There were small plates of food that people seemed to be enjoying. Finger food mostly, and veggies that nearly everyone ate from, as well as cold drinks. The cake had yet to be cut, and he almost hated to do that. It was a piece of art, and George and the rest of them had really outdone themselves with it.

Josh never left Carter's side. He held her hand when they spoke to people, or held her in his arms when they were just walking around. Introducing her to the people there gave him such a feeling of pride that he found himself taking her to see some people he'd not seen in years, just to show her off to them.

When it came time for them to cut the cake, he had his mom call the staff out to be there for them. George had been in and out of the room since they arrived, filling platters back up, replacing ones that were empty. There were servers all over the rooms, helping people with their coats and taking gifts to the other room.

"I got married today." Everyone laughed, just as he wanted them to. "I could not have had such a beautiful wedding had it not been for George and all the staff that are here tonight. I think they did a wonderful job, and I'd like for you all to give them a round of applause."

They were clearly embarrassed, yet pleased. As they began to thank certain people, Carter spoke up. He knew just what she was going to say before she spoke, and watched his mom's reaction to it.

"Let's not forget Eve Whitfield, for making the wedding at the courthouse today lowkey. I hope I can depend on her to go over the top on our children's birthday parties, as well as any other holiday that she wants to." Carter blew her a kiss and then looked at him. "I love you."

"And I love you."

Cutting the cake was difficult. It really was a gorgeous creation. With the several tiers and small roses with buds, he thought that whoever made it should go into business making them. Then when they did cut into the creation, he was so happy to see that it wasn't the traditional kind of white cake, but a fruit and nut cake that he and Carter loved so much.

As pieces of it were handed out, he and Carter were to open four of the gifts on the table. He had no idea who had started that tradition, but he was glad for it tonight. There were so many boxes with ribbons and cards there that he was sure that it would take them hours to open them all.

The first gift that they opened was from his parents. They gave them the deed to the land he'd bought from them, as well as they paid off the construction loan on his home. It was such a wonderful and thoughtful gift that they both went and hugged them for it.

Grandda's was next, and when he opened it, he handed it to Carter. As she started to cry over the card and contents, Grandda came up to stand next to them. Josh choked up twice when he read what it was to everyone.

"He adopted her. Grandda is now her father, and he said...." He had to wipe at his face. "He said that she was his first daughter, and she had made him prouder than he could have thought possible. And that my grandma would have loved to have met her and all the other girls that have come to mean so much to him."

The next gift was from his brothers. It was cash that they could use on their honeymoon. He thanked them several times for it, and they told him it was nothing. To him and Carter, it was everything.

The last gift was the one from the pack. It was a letter mostly. It said that they would forever be a part of their pack, and that whenever they needed them, Nate would be there with his army of wolves behind him. There couldn't have been a better gift from Nate and the others. To know that they'd be safe no matter what happened.

He and Carter were getting ready to leave when Tanner approached them. He said that he'd not have bothered them, but he thought it was important enough to tell them before they left. Taking him into their study, he asked them to have a seat just as Flora came into the room as well. She smiled at Carter, then sat on her hand. She looked up at Carter before speaking.

"You are not human. And the powers that you have, they are from your parents. Your real parents, who have missed you." Carter said that her parents were dead. "Nay, my lady. You are fae. A princess fae."

Chapter 12

Carter asked her where she'd gotten her information. Flora didn't move off her hand, but continued to stare at her. When she didn't answer her, she looked to Tanner for them.

"You were born in a small hospital on an off road, one that is magically maintained. There shouldn't have been humans that could find the place, so we're not entirely sure how the Comptons were able to find it. Desperation, I would imagine, and their child was born a few scant moments after they arrived." Carter asked them how they knew this. "When I first saw you, and then again the day before yesterday, I could smell fae on you. So, when I asked Flora if she had been hanging out with you, she told me that she'd not. So I found something of yours, and after testing it by smelling it, I knew what you were. But not who you were."

"I'm a human that has these incredible abilities." Flora told her that no human would be able to keep the amount of power that she had and still live. It would have killed a human the first time that they used it. "Then how do I have

173

them? I can't believe that anyone would believe that I'm not human."

"You are not only not a human, but you are the daughter of the queen of the fae's daughter. The granddaughter to the queen." Carter held tightly onto Josh's hand, and felt like she was in a washing machine, being tossed all around and not knowing which way was up. Tanner continued speaking as he sat down across from them. "I've spoken to the queen just today, and she is pleased that you have survived. Sadly, the daughter of the Comptons died not long after you were both born."

"I don't understand. Did they kidnap me?" Tanner said it was the fault of the clinic that they were switched at birth. "I'm not sure what is going on here. But I am just a human. I don't heal faster than anyone else, and I've been using my brain for all the stuff that I can do. The doctors, they told me that. That I used more of my brain than anyone else did."

"Perhaps you do. I wouldn't doubt that you use a great deal of it to control and use your magic. But that's what it is. The magic of your birth parents."

Carter stood up and started to pace the room. Josh asked how this had happened. She wanted to know as well.

"Why do you think they were switched at birth? Not that I don't believe you, but what happened?" Tanner started to tell them when Flora flew toward him and sat on his hand. He asked her the same question.

Carter didn't know how she felt right then. Overwhelmed by it all, certainly. But did she believe it? She wasn't sure if she did or not. It would certainly explain a great deal to her. But if it were true, her entire life had been a lie. Those people were not her parents. And this broke her heart the most, Rachel wasn't her sister, not by blood.

"They did not know what they had done. All these years they had thought they had done the right thing. But when the baby died only a few minutes after it was taken to the nursery, they all thought that it was the fae child and not the human." He asked why someone didn't feel the magic around Carter. "A child, as your wife would have been, would not have her magic until she was older. Eighteen in human years. She'd have some magic as she grew. And as I've been told, enough to get her into trouble with her parents. But not nearly what she has now. Everyone would feel it — they'd know that magic was close when she used it. But Carter was not in a place that it could be felt."

"The walls were made of concrete. And I only played with it in my cell." She came to sit by him again, and Josh kissed her and wiped away the tears that she'd shed. "The day I turned eighteen, I felt like my body had been turned inside out. I was sick for several days afterwards and had to be put in the infirmary. They told me that I had contracted some kind of virus, and that once I was well, they'd send me back to my cell. I've never been sick since."

"No, you'd not be. Nor would you die. Even before you came to be Josh's mate. When you're hurt, you don't heal faster, but anything that would have killed a lesser being would have just healed for you. To a certain point. You still have magic that will come to you from the queen and your parents." Carter told Tanner that she didn't want anything else that would change her. "I'm afraid, my dear, that regardless of your feelings for more magic, it will come to you because they know you are alive."

"What happened to the other child? The Compton baby?"

Tanner looked at Josh before he glanced at her. "Please tell me. I need to know more about this before I can come to terms with it all."

"The child wasn't healthy before it was born. Had it lived, I'm afraid that it would have been put someplace that was better able to handle a child like the one born to them. She had a great many birth defects, and her brain was very underdeveloped." Carter asked Tanner if he knew why that had happened. "Yes. And if the Comptons were alive when I found out the way they treated that unborn child of theirs, I would have gladly killed them again. But they would have suffered in ways that I have not used on humans before."

His voice was cold and hard. Carter didn't ask him what he'd do. The chill that ran over her body was enough to tell her that she didn't want to know. When Flora went to stand on the arm of the couch she was on, Carter put out her hand for her to walk onto. She was the most beautiful creature she had ever seen.

"She wishes to see you soon. Today if you would not mind." Carter looked at Josh, who smiled at her. "You are her granddaughter, and that makes you the most special child in the world to her."

"Where is her daughter? My mother? And my father?" Flora looked so sad. "They died? My parents are gone, and I won't get to meet them too?"

"Nay, they cannot die. But when they thought that their child had died, they asked to be put to rest. They have a grand faerie garden, the two of them do. And the queen, once she is certain that you are their daughter, she will ask them to wake. I'm sure that they'll wish that as well." Josh held her then—it was too much for her, and she sobbed. "I am sorry, my lady, but she will see what we all do. That you are her grandchild. I promise you."

"Flora, can you ask the queen to come here now? I don't think we should wait on an answer." Carter held onto Josh as he spoke quietly to the little fae. "I know that she has a great deal to do, but this is important to all of us, don't you think?"

"Yes, I'll go to her now." When the little fae left them out the small opening at the window, Carter looked at Tanner. He did not look like a man who had just brought good news to a lot of people. He was frighteningly pissed off looking. She asked him if he was upset that she might be the fae princess.

"Oh no. Never that. But there will be changes made to your life. I'm afraid that even if you tell her no, the moment that she sees you and confirms it, the magic will come to you regardless of your wants. But I was thinking of the other child. The one that should have been given to the Comptons, and I think that they would have ended her life without a qualm at all." She asked him if it would hurt her, the magic, trying hard not to think of what the Comptons would have done to their own child. And Tanner was right, they would have killed her. "No. I don't think so. You have a great deal of magic now. More than I think you were given at birth. And that is more than likely due to the fact that you honed your skills to the point that you gathered more from those around you. Not stole it, but used it as would have been your right."

"What happens to me should she figure out that I'm not related to her at all? Will she hurt me then?" He laughed and said that she'd never do that to a creature such as her. "I don't know what that means."

"If you are not the child that she seeks, then you are something that has well beyond the power of one so young.

She will wish to help you, perhaps groom you in a way that will help not just you, but herself as well." Carter asked him how. "I'm not sure. But she is at a point in her life, she told us, that she grows weary of her job. Not that she would ever show it to others, but she wishes…I guess you would say, she wishes to retire. And with her own daughter resting as she is, then there is no one to take over the duties of her life."

"Why did they not just have another child? I mean, it's been twenty-seven years. Couldn't they have had another child that would have been truly theirs?" Tanner shook his head and then stood up abruptly. She and Josh did as well.

The room brightened then dimmed, just before a woman appeared in the room with them. She was dressed in sparklers, it looked like to her, from the top of her head to her feet. Wings covered in gems spread out behind her, and when the light hit them, as it was now, there were sparks from it all around the room. When she staggered slightly, Carter didn't even hesitate but went to her aid. As soon as they touched, Carter felt a profound connection.

"You look so much like my daughter that I could mistake you for her." The touch to her cheek was soft, but no less charged full of energy. "You are her. My granddaughter. I can feel it, can't you?"

"I don't know what I feel. This has been a lot to take in." The men that were with the queen made themselves known to her. When they moved toward her, their swords drawn, Carter was afraid they were going to hurt one of them. "Stop."

Not one moved, but they did look to the queen when she started laughing. It was hardy and full of mirth. When she sat down on the other couch next to Tanner, the queen took Carter's hand into her much smaller one.

"If I had my doubts before, which I did not, this proves it, don't you think?" Tanner nodded at the queen, but Carter was confused. "She can command my army, Tanner. Did you know this when you invited me here, my dear friend?"

"I did not." They both looked at her, and Tanner asked her to have a seat. "You see, only a royal can command the guard of the queen. When you told them to stop moving, they had no choice but to do as you commanded. Had you not been the one that we thought, they would have run you through to save their queen. You are most assuredly the granddaughter of the queen of the fae."

Carter returned to Josh and he held her in his arms. She wanted a few minutes to absorb all this. And there was a great deal of it to take in. She wasn't human, for starters. Not only was that piece of news too much, but it turned out that she was the granddaughter to the queen of all the fae in the world. Her mind went sideways for a second, and she had a thought that the queen would be commanding them on other planets too. When she felt like she could settle into her thoughts again, she had about sixty billion questions that were circling around in her noodle.

"Are you all right?" She wasn't sure and told Josh that. It was then that she realized that they were alone in the big room. "They said that they'd be back when we came home from our honeymoon. But the queen did leave you a couple of pieces of jewelry that she'd like for us both to wear."

The ring was just a plain band, until she put it on her finger. Then it was not only just as gem covered as the queen's wings were, but seemed to glow with a light as bright as the fucking sun. Wearing it could bring attention to her, and she wasn't sure that she'd like that any more than knowing that her life had been one lie after another.

"I'm not thinking straight right now." Josh laughed. "You must think I'm an idiot. I've been told that those horrible people weren't my parents, and I'm acting stupid."

"No, I think you're reacting to a great deal of information that has been thrown at you all at once. I also would never think that you're stupid." She was trying to pull the ring off her finger, but it wasn't budging. "It won't come off. She said that it marked you as who you are, and it will keep you safe. I have one as well. As husband to the granddaughter of the queen, I must be safe as well."

"You're enjoying this, aren't you?" He laughed and said it was strange, but better than he thought it would be. "Yes, well, I'm not so sure about the better part. But it is different. What do we do now? I mean, are we going away like we thought we were?"

"Oh yes. Everything is arranged. The car is waiting on us to take us to the airport. The only difference that I can see to our plans is that we'll have a few extra men around us at all times to keep us safe." She asked him why. "You're her granddaughter, and the moment she acknowledged you, you became important to her. And to me, if you want the truth of it. You've always been very important to me."

"You just like getting laid on a regular basis, that's why you find me important." He laughed and took her hand into his. "We're leaving, just like we planned, right? I don't think I could take one more thing to be different right now, Josh. Let's go and have a wonderful honeymoon."

"I promise you, it will be the best honeymoon anyone has ever been on." He kissed her then. "I love you, Mrs. Carter Whitfield. With all my heart."

Josh knew that he should have told her the rest, what she'd gained by wearing the ring—what he'd gained as well. But he didn't want Carter stressed out any more than she was already. It had been a hell of a month since she'd come into his life, and he needed for her to enjoy herself. When they returned, there would be a great many more changes that would have to be dealt with. He remembered, in great detail, what the queen had told him while Carter was in his arms and overawed.

"My daughter and her husband will be awakened as soon as I go back to the castle. There are things there that must be prepared for the two of you." Josh had asked her what that would be. "You will be able to go between your home here and the one at the castle without any trouble. The magic that is hers, it will be given to you as well. Only less. You'll still have a great deal, Josh, but she will need more."

"I understand. I do have a question, if I may?" She nodded at him. "Why didn't they just have another child? I mean, I'm assuming that she's older than me, but there would have been time for them to have another child."

"Our kind, the royalty of the fae, can only have a single birth. It will be born a girl child, and she will be in direct line to the throne when the time comes." Josh told her that he was so sorry about that. "It's the way that it has been forever. I knew this when I had my own daughter, and she the same."

"So, you not only lost your granddaughter in all this, but your daughter as well." She had smiled sadly at him and said that was right. "I'll talk to Carter, but when the time is right, my lady. She hasn't had a good life up until now, and I have promised her that we'd take this trip. I wish, for you, the timing could have been much better. But she's not been sleeping well, and I want her to be less stressed so that she can."

"I will not harm her, Josh, but I will help her with her sleep. I'm to understand that she has nightmares?" He said that she had them almost nightly. "I will give her a bit of my magic so that she can also rest while she is away. It will be good for you both to try and relax while you are having this trip. And please don't think of this as me losing my daughter and hers too. I have gained them both back this day, and I have never been happier."

And now they were on a plane headed to the first leg of their journey. Carter was restless, he knew that, and when she finally turned to him, he could tell that his telling her later thought was out the window. She was readier for what he knew than she had been before.

After telling her everything that he knew, she leaned back on the seat and looked at the seat across from her. He'd bet that she wasn't seeing what was there, but thinking and processing all that he'd told her. He even told her about the child that they'd have, and how it would only be the one.

"Can we adopt more children?" He told her he'd love that. "I'm trying to think around all this information, so I'm sorry if it comes out a little scattered."

"That's quite all right. I don't know that I'd be any less scattered if I had just had all this told to me." She looked at him and he smiled. "You're very beautiful when you're confused, did you know that?"

"I'm going to hurt you." He laughed and was glad when she did as well. "What did she mean about going to the castle?"

"I'm assuming that she lives in one with a lot of other people. But where it is, I've no idea. I guess that's smart on their part, not to let just anyone know. She was going to wake her daughter when she returned. I'm not sure how that works or how long it might take, but she said to expect her to pop in once or twice. It would be harder on her, I think. Thinking that you were dead all this time." Carter nodded and asked him about the ring. "It's to protect us both. The only beings that can see it for what it is are other paranormals. And you remember me telling you about the guards? Well, they'll be around to keep anyone from hurting us as well."

"I went from being an ex-con—well, sort of—to being a fae princess married to the best man I know." Josh thanked her for that. "Now, what aren't you telling me?"

"There is money that belongs to us now." She said that she'd signed all the paperwork before they were wed. "No, this is from the queen. Riches beyond our wildest dreams, I think she called it."

"Okay, overwhelmed again. Where are we going to be staying tonight?" Josh told her of the house that Tanner had set up for them to see to first. "Really? It's in France? I've only seen pictures of the place, and I'm betting that they don't do it justice."

"I've been there once or twice. Mostly to see to something for the family." She told him how when she'd graduated from high school she'd planned to go too. "I'm assuming that because of the Comptons you were unable to go."

"Yes, and they were able to get to my money too. Even though I'd graduated from high school the year before, I had a job working at the mall." She laughed then. "When I think of all the shit that they pulled on Rachel and me, all I can think about is how they had these grand plans that were taken away from them just like they took it all from me."

The laughter wasn't supposed to be funny. She was bitter about them, and who could blame her. They had taken a great deal from her. And they would have done a lot more had they lived. Even Rachel was better now that they were gone, and seemed to be living her life to the fullest.

"Do they have a name?" It took his mind a moment to come back to the subject of the queen and her daughter. "I mean, do I call them Grandma Queen and Mom Princess?"

"I don't think that would work anyway. But in answer to your question, yes, they all have names. Your grandmother's name is Breen. Your mother's name is Sennetta. And your father's name is Raytheon. As you can imagine, they've no last names. Your father wasn't human when he married your mom, but he wasn't fae either. I believe Breen said that he was a leader of the brownie warriors. They met when he saved Sennetta from being kidnapped one day."

Josh and Carter bounced back and forth between what they were going to do on their honeymoon to what else Breen had told him. There was a great deal of information on the latter yet to be told, but she was content with hearing it in small doses, and he was fine with that too. When she finally got around to the rings, he was prepared for her questions.

"You said that they're only seen by other paranormals. What about humans that want to hurt us? I'm sure that there will be some, aren't you?"

He told her just what he'd been told. "There isn't a weapon in the entire universe that can harm either of us. Or any children that we might bring into our lives." She asked him if that meant adopting. "I'm assuming so. I didn't ask. I

184

was more focused on the fact that my poor wife was sobbing on my chest and I couldn't fix it."

When Carter came and sat on his lap, he held her. She told him that he had fixed it by loving her. It was the nicest answer she could have given him. When she finally dozed off, he held her for as long as he could before the plane was ready to stop on the first part of their journey. His dad contacted him as they were going down the tarmac.

I thought you should know that your house is being overrun. He asked him with what. *The most uniformly dressed little faeries that I've ever seen. There must be millions of them. They're painting the house a nice shade of light green, and your shutters, which I don't think you had before, are a deep brown. It looks very nice. I can't tell what they're doing on the inside as yet. I'm sort of afraid to go and look.*

Josh told his dad what he could. Nothing about Carter — he didn't know how to tell that other than face to face. But he did tell him that they would be home in a month, and to keep him updated.

Some papers are going to come to you at your house. They're for Carter and me. If you could take care that they are at the house when we get there, I'd really appreciate it. And Tanner may look you up for a couple of things he'd like for you to do for him. Dad said he'd do whatever he needed. *I told him you'd say that. It's not huge, but something to do with daylight hours, and he can't do that when the man can meet him. I guess you'll get the information sometime in the next couple of days for you to help him.*

All right. How is your pretty bride today? I'm telling you, that is one heck of a girl you got there. All that power in her, and her being just a little bitty thing too. Josh told him she was learning to handle it. *I think she does really well now. And you tell her that*

I said so.

I will, Dad. And I love you. I don't tell you that often enough, I don't think. Dad said that he didn't, none of them did, but it was nice to hear it from him. *I'll make sure that they tell you more often if you'll give us a call when you need to be told. It'll be my pleasure.*

When the limo that met them at the airport pulled up in front of a large house and servants were lined up waiting for them, Josh got out, laughing. This trip would not be boring, he thought, as he handed Carter out of the car too.

Chapter 13

Adam sat down on his couch and tried to think what he could do now. He'd rearranged his cabinets, cleaned out the pantry, and had dusted the entire house from top to bottom. It was like this every year when he put his big boy toys away and had too much energy to just sit around the house. His house would get a total cleaning, and he'd be worn out enough to sleep at night. Laughing, he got up to answer the door when someone knocked.

He wasn't sure who he expected to be there, but to see his mom was something that had him startled into silence. When she asked him if he was all right, he asked her the same.

"Can't a mom come and see her little boy?" He asked her when she had ever used the front door to the houses of her sons, and then knocked too. "I'm trying to be more mom like and not the nosey biddy sort. What are you doing this fine day?"

"Its pouring down rain. What's going on?" She huffed at him and came into the house. Adam followed her to his living room and took her coat from her when she held it out. "I don't think you're a nosey biddy, by the way."

"It's taken you long enough to say that, don't you think?" He sat down in the easy chair that he'd kept from his Grandda's things. "I'm not going to snip at you anymore."

"I don't care so long as I know why I'm being snipped at. Have I forgotten something? Done something that I don't remember?" She shook her head. "Then why are you snipping at me? And everyone else. That's why you're here, isn't it? You've over-snipped your welcome elsewhere."

"What a thing to say to your own mother." She looked ready to cry. "You don't need me anymore."

The dam opened up and she started sobbing. Going to her, he held her while she cried out her reason for being so mean to everyone.

"You all have your own homes that you keep nice. I have two grandsons that are in school all day, so I can't be with them. Sunny is going to have her baby soon, and she's all prepared with it all. She does ask me questions, but I think she knows the answer and is humoring me." He told her that no one was humoring her. "But you don't need me anymore, do you, Adam?"

He pulled her chin up so that she could look at him before speaking. "Mom, I will forever need you. I need you to be there for me every day. And while I might not come to you for help every day, I do like knowing that you're right there should I need you. You are my rock and my foundation. There isn't a day that goes by that I don't think of you a million times. What would Mom think of this? Or, what would Mom do in this situation? And every time, you give me the right answers and the right path to stay on. Even when you're not around me."

"That's what I needed to hear." She was still crying, so he asked her what was wrong now. "I'm so happy."

Women were weird. He'd had an idea that they were before his mom came to see him today. He still didn't know why, but women were all weird, and he was going to avoid them at all costs.

Adam wasn't sure how he was going to make that happen yet. When your mate was out there just waiting to pounce, you had no choice in the matter. And the only way that he could make this work, he thought, was to sell everything he owned, buy an island, and stay on it alone for the rest of his life. But with his luck, she'd be swimming out in the ocean and come by his place to have a rest or something.

He didn't really have any qualms about having a mate. They were a good thing, he supposed. His brothers sure did seem to be happy. And the thought that they'd turned mushy was sort of funny. Adam had never thought of himself as a romantic type of man, but he supposed neither had his brothers. And they seemed to be doing all right.

"What's going on in that head of yours?" Instead of telling her nothing, he told her everything that he'd been thinking about. "Women are not weird. And that's not a very nice thing to say. What would you do if Dylan, Sunny, or Carter heard you?"

"I'd be more worried about what they'd do to me and not what I said to them." She laughed when he did. "I don't know why that thought popped into my head. I was thinking how strange it is that you, and I don't mean just you, but all women have the emotions of a two-year-old. Sad? You cry. You're thrilled to death about something? You cry. I don't know how other men handle that up and down stuff all the time."

She sat up, and he was worried that he'd offended her or something. But when she spoke, she was telling him what it was with women, or her version of it, she told him.

"We do, I suppose, have the emotions of a child, but we love someone with all that we are. And we take the love to the grave with us. But men handle the ups and downs very well when they love someone as much as they're loved back." She ran her hand over his cheek, then slapped him. It wasn't painful, but he knew that she could have made it very painful should she have wanted. "And do not ever call me a two-year-old again."

"Yes, ma'am." He smiled at her. "I guess when the time comes, I'll be able to love someone as much as I do you. But I can't imagine me being all mushy like the others are. I mean, they'll lay down their lives for their mates."

"As you will." He didn't think so, but didn't want to get slapped again, more than likely harder. "I was feeling the loss of my baby boys today. I just needed to have one of you say that you might need me for a little while longer. And you go and tell me that you're not sure that I'm an adult. I do hope you have better manners with your mate when the time comes."

"I hope so as well. If she's anything like the other three in the family, I'll be dead and pushing up pretty flowers for you to water in no time." She laughed when he did. "I know that having a mate will change me. I'm aware that I'll love her beyond anything that I ever have before, but why?"

"What do you mean, why? You love her because she loves you. And you'll be spending the rest of your life wanting her to be happy and cherished. Don't you want that?" He told her that he didn't know. "Oh, poor Adam. When she gets here, I'm going to have such fun watching the two of you come together."

"I don't want her to change me." She frowned at him. "The others, they've made changes in their lives to suit their mates. Not that they're not happy, they really look like they are. But I'm a rancher, Mom. A person that gets up when the cows do and goes to bed shortly after the sun has left the sky. How does anyone expect me to court and woo a woman when I have more work going on than most?"

"Perhaps this woman that comes to you, she'll like ranching as well." He just huffed at her. "Well, she could. Or she'll be one of those frou-frou girls, and you'll have to cater to her every whim so that you'll be able to get laid once in a while. I don't know."

Adam hugged his mom as he laughed with her. "You have my heart, Mom. I don't know if I have anything left for a woman other than you."

"You'll see, Adam. When she comes, it'll all work out, and you'll be sorry that you ever stressed so much about it." He told her that he supposed so. "Not to mention, when she does get here, she might make you get rid of all the furniture in this house and buy new. Even your grandda is surprised that you still have it in here. Don't you care for change?"

"I don't, actually. But that's not why I've not done anything to it. I love the smells that are here. I can still smell Grandma on some of the sheets that I put on the beds. The handmade quilts that she made, when I touch them, I can see her bent over the quilting frame putting beautiful designs all over the top of it. And Grandda's chair holds me like he did when I was younger and would scrape my knee or something." She told him that was romantic. "Naw. It's also expensive to buy new stuff when I have all this around. Not to mention, until last week, I was working from dawn to dusk, and had no time to mess with it."

"It's a good thing that I love you, Adam, or I'd beat your bottom until you couldn't sit for a month. The things that spill from that mouth of yours borders on meanness." She kissed him on the cheek as she stood up. "Well, I must go and find Blake and Adrian. They'll need their mother to talk them out of being a fool when their mates come. I'm afraid there is no hope for you and yours. She'll just have to come here and see what a mess you are. And she'll blame it all on me."

"No, she won't. I won't let her. She'll be nice to you or I'll lock her in the shed out back." She tisked at him again as she took her coat from him. "Or, I could do what I was thinking anyway. Buy myself an island and live out my days as a hermit. Eating fish all day that I catch and cook on an open fire."

"You do that, and I will beat you senseless. Not that I don't think you are now."

With another kiss she went out the door and waved at him from her car. Adam loved his mom so very much.

The rest of his morning was spent on finding something to fill the living room with. Grandda's chair did hug him, but it also had a nasty spring in it that would catch him unaware sometimes and he'd have to carefully get up off the thing. There was also a need for him to get a few lamps. There wasn't an overhead light, and he found the room to be too dark sometimes.

He thought about a television. Adam only watched

football on it, and when he could a baseball game. There were really small ones that he could carry from room to room with him to watch, but he decided that he wanted huge to watch the games with his family and think they were right on the fifty-yard line. As he made his list of things he wanted, he also looked for things on the Internet. He hated shopping almost as much as he hated being without something to do.

By the time he had placed an order to be delivered, he was ready for his lunch. Not that there was much in the place—he'd been much too busy to hit the stores other than to grab some milk and eggs. That was another list that he started as he made himself a peanut butter sandwich. Not only with the last of the peanut butter, but he had no jelly, nor any bread left. He'd have to hit up Mom's house today to replenish his jelly stash.

Going into town in the driving rain, he was careful of the road. A lot of the trees had lost all their color over the last two days, and it was slick on the road with all the rain. As he was pulling up in front of the market to get his food, he saw an elderly man struggling to get in his wheel chair and then into the store. Helping him do both, Adam asked him if he needed help shopping.

"No, I got it, young man. I was trying to hurry, and that never works out for me." He laughed with the man. "You go on about your business. I've been flirting with one of the cashiers here, and she'll help me out just fine."

Adam wished him luck and got a cart. Another domestic thing that he hated doing was food shopping. All of it sounded really good while here, but he'd get home and wonder why he'd purchased such a thing. Maybe his future mate would like to shop. That might be something that he could put on the pro side of his mental list.

After finishing up with his list and grabbing several jars of jelly from Dad, as Mom was still out, he headed home. Putting away the groceries, he'd thought he'd done well until he got to the bottom of the bag. Why the hell had he purchased a leg of lamb? He didn't even know how to cook it.

~~~

Meghan hated everything about this little town that they'd stopped in. But the car had needed to be fixed, and since she wasn't going to do it, there had to be someone out there that would. As soon as her sister came back to the little room that she was in, she asked her how long this was going to take.

"Do I look like a mechanic to you? I told you when you went on this harebrained idea of yours that this wasn't going to work. Your car is older than I am, and you don't even drive. What the hell do you even have it for? Not to mention, you didn't make any plans other than to make me drive you to the coast. The coast, in case you didn't know, is a pretty fucking big place." Ivy sat down in the room's only chair, and that pissed Meghan off too. "You'll have to find us a room for the night. He said that he has to order parts, and they'll be here either tomorrow or the next day."

"What do you mean, find *us* a room? You find your own room." Ivy glared at her. "Well, I'm not paying for you to have a room too. You'll have to sleep in the car if you don't have the money for it."

Ivy stood up and Meghan took a step back. She hated that her sister was so much taller than her. Thinner and in better shape too. Meghan would have killed for a body like Ivy's, but she'd never tell her that. She liked having her sister

194

envious of her.

"I didn't want to come on this trip at all. You told me that it was urgent that you get to the coast, a matter of life and death. Now, nearly two hundred miles into this, you tell me that you needed to be on the beach someplace that would give you a natural tan. You will pay for me a room, or I'll take the next flight home and leave you here. Now do it."

Meghan started to tell her to try it, but was afraid that she would do just as she said. Just lately, Ivy had gotten all up in her grill about things. She fussed at her about unpaid bills and how her apartment wasn't clean enough. Meghan was depressed, and when she was depressed, all she wanted to do was eat and sleep. Not necessarily a good combination, but she had been doing it that way since she'd gotten her heart broken by Timmy Coates when she'd been seven. He'd told her that he didn't like her hair, and that was it for him.

Unlike Ivy, Meghan's hair was pin straight and brown. Not any nice color like honey or even tan, but a nondescript brown. Ivy's hair was fire engine red, and as curly as if she'd just had a perm the day before. She didn't wear makeup either, just went into the stores and mall without so much as a bit of lip color on her face.

Meghan wouldn't go anywhere without fixing her face and hair. It was why Ivy would get so frustrated with her, she was always late and vain. She knew this about herself, but she had no desire to change herself. Someday, she knew, it would get her a husband, and she'd be as happy as she'd ever been.

If her parents' marriage was any indication of how marital bliss was, she was going to be sadly disappointed. They had married young, had her and then Ivy, then divorced each other. Now they both had been married again a total of six times between them. And her and Ivy had so many half, step, and whatever else could be thrown in the pot as siblings. They rarely saw them or their parents anymore. Probably due to them being so broke all the time.

Meghan had money. Not a great deal of it like Ivy did, but she had enough to do what she wanted. Her ambition was to have been a doctor someday. But her first time in one of the classes where she had to do math, she'd dropped out. It had been like that her whole life. Dropping out of things. She supposed that was what made Ivy upset with her.

Ivy did well at whatever she set her mind to. Of course, she did become a doctor, and was very good at it. And right now, she was on her month off which she took every year to get her home in order. Which she owned as well. Meghan thought that she could really hate her sister.

But she didn't. She loved her so much that she ached with it at times. And now she had upset her again by being selfish. She went to call the town's only place to stay, and was given two rooms at a discount. Apparently it was off season for them, and they were glad to have the guests. Then she went to find Ivy.

She was down on the floor giving CPR to the mechanic. Meghan rushed to her side to find out what she could do to help her. Ivy told her to call nine-one-one, and to tell them that a doctor was on site.

Meghan made the call and tried to calm her pounding heart when she was told that an ambulance was on the way and that there was a doctor coming as well. An Evan Whitfield was their local doctor when he was in town. All she knew to tell them was the name of the mechanic shop, and they knew just where they were.

Ivy never stopped what she was doing, even though Meghan knew she had to be exhausted. She was just watching her. And when the sirens started to blare closer to them, she asked her sister if she needed anything.

"No. I have it." She was panting hard, and there was a strain to her shoulders and back. She could see the bunched-up muscles with every compression that she did. And when the doctor from the ambulance came into the garage, he moved to take over without missing a single beat. It was as well planned at it looked. Ivy leaned back on her ass and told the doctor what she'd encountered when she came to talk to him.

"He was on his knees, just falling over when I saw him. He told me that he was having heart pains all day." Dr. Whitfield told them that he was a candidate for a heart valve, but wouldn't do it because of the cost. "I see that a great deal where I work as well. I suppose dying to these people isn't as bad."

"That's about the right of it." They traded off again while the medics came into the room with all their equipment. "You're a physician?"

"Yes."

Ivy glanced at her, and Meghan knew that she wasn't to say what sort of doctor her sister was. Heart replacement was her specialty, but she did all kinds of heart operations. She was a renowned surgeon that everyone knew about.

Once the medics took over, both doctors stood back while things were being taken care of. Mr. Williams, it seemed, was going to be in big trouble if he refused the surgery again, and Evan, as he told them both to call him, said he was going to have to do some fast talking to his wife before the gentleman woke up.

Less than two hours later, not only was Ivy scrubbing in with the good doctor, but Meghan sat with the very nice wife of Evan. Ivy was less than happy about the situation. Not that she blamed her. Ivy had recently had some trouble at home that was haunting her.

"Your sister is a good doctor then?" Meghan, proud to be talking about her sister, told her who she was. "I'm not sure if I know the name, but then I usually avoid doctors when I can. Except for Evan, I'm pretty much out of the loop. And before I forget to tell you, Evan told me to tell you that you and your sister are more than welcome to stay with us until your car is fixed. Mr. Williams might be down for a bit."

"We have a place at the B&B." The woman nodded and got up, saying she was going to get herself something to eat, and Meghan joined her when asked. "I'm afraid that Ivy isn't going to be any happier about this trip than she was before. I sort of tricked her into coming with me. I just needed to get away. And while I'd like to say that she did as well, she won't see it that way."

"Evan knows your sister. Or at least of her. She lost a patient recently." Meghan wondered how she knew that, but didn't ask. "I'm sorry that she's having a hard time of it. Evan goes into a funk when he loses one too."

"Do you know how long this surgery will last? I'm exhausted, and I'd like to go back to the place we're staying." Dylan asked her about her sister. "She knows where it is, and she'll need to take a run afterwards. It blows off the adrenalin after she comes out of the operating room. She might not even come back until the wee hours of the morning."

"I can drop you off then."

Thanking her, Meghan gathered her things and the little bit that Ivy had, and followed the woman to the car. She seemed upset about something, and Meghan was too tired to figure it out. As soon as she was in her room after letting the owner know that Ivy would be in later, she was glad for the big bed.

It was six thirty in the morning when Ivy woke her. Trying to make her slow down on what she was saying finally had her snapping at her again. When she was finally awake, she looked at Ivy and immediately felt bad for yelling at her, and asked what had happened.

"My house is gone." That made no sense to her, and she asked her what she was talking about. "Someone broke into it sometime yesterday and burned it to the ground. There is nothing left. I lost everything I own."

"Oh Ivy, I'm so sorry. What can I do to help you?" She told her nothing, she was sorry for waking her. "No, that's all right. I'm sorry that I've been such a bitch to you. What did they say caused it?"

Instead of answering her, she handed her the paper. The fax paper had been crumbled up and stained a little, but she could read it well enough. It was a note from the man who had burned her house down; he'd sent it to the police station over three hours ago.

"Dr. Ivy Walton, see how it is to lose everything in your life. I'm not finished with you yet. Signed, David Cooper."

"I have nothing to go back to now. I have my job, of course, but I've been dissatisfied with that for some time. I'm thinking that once you get to your coast, I'll stick around there. No point in going home again when I have nothing there." Meghan told her that she couldn't do that, she'd miss her. "I'll have a phone, Meghan. This is what I need to do. To start fresh. Hopefully since he signed his handiwork, he'll be caught. After this, he's in a lot of trouble, I would suppose. But I'm not going back."

When she left her in favor of her own room, Meghan wondered what she was to do now. This trip, while starting out for her own selfish reasons, had really turned into something to help Ivy. And now she was going to leave her. Well, Meghan wasn't going to allow that to happen. She needed her sister. Meghan would figure out something, and this time follow through on it. Ivy wasn't leaving her.

Before You Go...

HELP AN AUTHOR

write a review

THANK YOU!

Share your voice and help guide other readers to these wonderful books. Even if it's only a line or two your reviews help readers discover the author's books so they can continue creating stories that you'll love. Login to your favorite retailer and leave a review. Thank you.

AWARD WINNING, BESTSELLING AUTHOR

Kathi Barton, winner of the Pinnacle Book Achievement award as well as a best-selling author on Amazon and All Romance books, lives in Nashport, Ohio with her husband Paul. When not creating new worlds and romance, Kathi and her husband enjoy camping and going to auctions. She can also be seen at county fairs with her husband who is an artist and potter.

Her muse, a cross between Jimmy Stewart and Hugh Jackman, brings her stories to life for her readers in a way that has them coming back time and again for more. Her favorite genre is paranormal romance with a great deal of spice. You can visit Kathi online and drop her an email if you'd like. She loves hearing from her fans. aaronskiss@gmail.com.

Follow Kathi on her blog: http://kathisbartonauthor. blogspot.com/